ANNIE'S CHOICE

Clara Gillow Clark

BOYDS MILLS PRESS

To my mother, for her years of selfless giving

The author wishes to give special thanks to Bunny Gabel and Patricia Reilly Giff for all their support and encouragement during the writing of this novel.

––––––

COPYRIGHT © 1993 BY CLARA GILLOW CLARK
JACKET ILLUSTRATION COPYRIGHT © 1993 BY BOYDS MILLS PRESS
ALL RIGHTS RESERVED

PUBLISHED BY CAROLINE HOUSE
BOYDS MILLS PRESS, INC.
A HIGHLIGHTS COMPANY
815 CHURCH STREET
HONESDALE, PENNSYLVANIA 18431
PRINTED IN THE UNITED STATES OF AMERICA

PUBLISHER CATALOGING-IN-PUBLICATION DATA
Clark, Clara Gillow.
        Annie's choice / Clara Gillow Clark.
[200]p. : cm.
Summary: Living in the 1920s, Annie must decide whether to go on to high school or stay at home to help her family.
ISBN: 1-56397-053-8
1. United States—History—1919-1933—Juvenile fiction.
[1. United States—History—1919-1933—Fiction.] I. Title.
        [F]   1993
Library of Congress Catalog Card Number: 91-77602 CIP

FIRST EDITION, 1993
BOOK DESIGNED BY JEANNE ABBOUD
THE TEXT OF THIS BOOK IS SET IN 12-POINT GARAMOND.
DISTRIBUTED BY ST. MARTIN'S PRESS

10 9 8 7 6 5 4 3 2 1

Annie's Choice

1993

For Sarah,

Warmest wishes to a fellow
book lover!

Chris Gillow Chant

ONE

A nnie Lucas clenched her teeth and bore down on the scrub brush. One thing she knew for certain, she was *never* going to get married, and she *wasn't* going to have a bunch of babies. Mom already had more than her share . . . Mae and Russell and Annie and Ben and Leo and Grace. Mom was tuckered out all the time.

"Ow!" Annie sat back on her heels and flung the scrub brush into the pail of water. A long splinter from the wood floor was run clean under the skin of her middle finger.

It was awful enough emptying the chamber pots each morning, but Ben and Leo were always missing or sloshing the pot when they shoved it beneath the bed. Seemed she was scrubbing and wiping up their floor every day. It just wasn't fair.

Annie pushed at the splinter with her thumb. She hated Saturdays. There was no school to look forward to, only chores and more chores the whole day. Annie couldn't wait till she was old enough to leave home. She was in eighth grade now, but Mom would never allow her to work in the factory in town till she was at least fifteen, and that was pretty near two years away.

Annie fished the brush out of the pail and began scrubbing slowly. She never tired of dreaming about what she would do then—the things she'd buy, the places she'd go. . . . Her older sister, Mae, used to be full of stories of town life when she came home for a visit, but all Mae talked about now was Elmer and getting married. It was enough to make a body sick. "Why would you go and do a fool thing like getting married? You'll end up with a whole passel of babies just like Mom," Annie would say to Mae.

Mae would only laugh. "Oh, Annie, that's purely silly. You don't know the first thing about it."

"Mail for Miss Annie Lucas!" Annie's daydream was interrupted by Uncle Elton, their mailman, who stood out on the porch.

She dropped the scrub brush, wiped her hands on her dress, and fled down the stairs. Now what mail could she be getting? Her birthday was long past.

Uncle Elton was inside, with Mom and the younger children swarming around him, when Annie hurried into the kitchen. Grace ran toward her and grabbed the folds of her skirt. "It's pretty, Annie," she said, her eyes wide with wonder.

"Stinks," Ben said, wrinkling his nose.

"Yeah, stinks," Leo echoed.

"Hush, boys. Mind your manners," Mom said.

Uncle Elton laughed and held a letter out to Annie.

The envelope was pink and smelled of rose sachet. Annie stared at her name, her heart pounding.

Miss Annie Lucas
Rural Delivery
South Branch, New York

Annie longed to rush down to the outhouse and shut herself in. It was the only place she could go for quiet. At the house there was always such a crowd around that a body couldn't get a minute's peace.

Ben shoved her elbow. "Hurry up, Annie. I want to know what it's about."

Annie ignored him. If Uncle Elton and Mom hadn't been there, she'd have pinched him good and hard. She couldn't wait until those pesky boys were old enough to help out with the barn chores every day.

But they all stood and waited. They'd stare at her the whole blessed day, waiting until she opened it. Annie slit the envelope and glanced over the letter quickly before reading it aloud.

October 8, 1928

Dear Annie,

I would be most delighted if you would join me for luncheon on Saturday, Seventeen October, Nineteen Hundred and Twenty-eight, at Eleven A.M. O'Clock. Please respond in person by school dismissal on Friday.

Sincerely yours,
Miss Olive Osborne

"It's from the teacher," Ben said with disgust. "Annie's the teacher's pet."

"Yeah, teacher's pet," Leo said.

"You boys leave Annie be," Mom said.

Yes, please, let me be, thought Annie. Her hands shook as she folded the letter and slid it back into the envelope. Miss Osborne was new this year and young —younger even than Mae. She'd come all the way from Stroudsburg, Pennsylvania, to teach here. "I want to go," Annie blurted out, pressing the letter against her chest. "Please, Mom, may I go?"

Mom never could make up her mind right off. She seemed thoughtful. "It might be all right," she said finally. She poked some stray wisps of graying hair up into her bun. "There'll be Saturday's chores all the same, but it's not for me to say. You'll have to ask your dad." Mom turned away from her. "How about a glass of cider before you get back to your route, Elton?" Mom said. "Warner and Russell pressed some yesterday. It's real sweet this year." She walked toward the pantry. Uncle Elton and the boys followed her.

Annie rushed upstairs to her room. It was a blessing just to get away and be left alone to finish her chores. She was free to think, at least. She went straight to her bureau and slid the letter under her bloomers. She'd take it out later when she was done with the work and read it clear through by herself. No one had ever invited just her by herself anywhere or written her a letter on paper smelling pretty like perfume.

"I saw where you hid that letter," Grace said.

Annie whirled around. Grace had her chin stuck out the way Ben would. She seemed always to know when something was meant to be special or private. "If you touch my letter, I'll break your arm."

Grace sniffed. Her eyes filled with tears.

"Now don't go crying like a baby," Annie said crossly. "I didn't mean it. Understand?"

Grace nodded. She looked about ready to bawl.

Annie went to the little girl and caught her up in a hug. Grace wrapped her arms around Annie's neck. Annie hated being cross with her. It was so hard not to love Grace.

"I won't tell nobody where you hid your letter, honest," Grace said.

Grace wouldn't mean to, anyway. But secrets were hard for Grace to keep. She loved to tell things.

Annie set her down. "I have to get my chores done, Grace. How about coming with me to empty the slop pail?" No sense taking a chance on Grace. Annie got her letter and slid it into the pocket of her dress before going to the boys' room for the pail.

As soon as she and Grace stepped out the pantry door, Grace caught sight of Ben and Leo playing on the big rocks in the pasture. Grace ran off down the path hollering, "Can I play?"

Annie walked across the yard to the outhouse and dumped the slops, then came slowly back to the house. It appeared that the boys and Grace were playing tag. Grace was making war whoops and chasing after Leo. For once the boys had let her play.

Annie stood on the back step and watched for a minute before pulling open the screen and going inside.

"That you, Annie?" Mom called from the kitchen.

"Yes, Mom," Annie said, setting the pail down by the pantry door and going to the basin to wash her hands. It was quiet in the house with the boys outside and even Grace not following her around. If she talked about the letter now, Mom might be persuaded to let her go.

"Get yourself a paring knife and help me with these apples," Mom called out.

Annie got a knife and went out to the kitchen. Mom was peeling apples from a bushel basket on the floor. "I'm working on pies for supper, but you can slice some apples for drying," Mom said as Annie pulled a chair over by the basket.

"I'm real pleased the teacher sent me that letter," Annie said, picking up an apple. "Nobody ever invited me anywhere before. It's real exciting."

"I suppose," Mom said. She shook her head and made a clucking sound. "It's peculiar about young'uns, how they can be so different even in the same family —like you and Mae. There's just no figuring. You got all the good sense and just keep right on doing your chores even though you got that piece of mail. Why, if that were Mae, she'd be trying on her Sunday clothes

and fretting over her looks, not one bit of help to me."
Mom sighed. "I prayed to the good Lord, 'Send me a
girl that has got some sense and will be a help.'
Couldn't have got no better one than you, Annie,"
Mom said.

Annie quartered an apple and cut the seeds out.
She should have been pleased with all the praise Mom
was piling on her, but she wasn't. Mom would say she
was acting like Mae if she started in begging to go.

"Your sister was not born for the likes of farm life,
that's for sure. I reckon that teacher of yours might
have the same fancy ideas, being a city girl." Mom laid
her knife on the table and gave Annie a long look.

"Miss Osborne is not like Mae. She's a *town* girl, but
she's not one bit flighty," Annie said, picking up
another apple.

"I guess it'd be too soon for you to be judging that,
Annie," Mom said. She stood up and took the bowl
heaped with apple slices off the table. "I'd better get
making the pies. You keep on peeling till you get the
big pot full." Mom cradled the bowl and went out to
the pantry.

Annie jabbed the knife into an apple. It was real
clear Mom didn't want her to go, and chances were, if
Mom said she couldn't spare Annie from Saturday's
chores, Dad would just go along. Dad was more pre-
dictable about things than Mom, but more firm, too.
No one tried persuading him different once his mind
was made up, but when it came to the children, it

seemed Mom always got the say.

Dad found out about her letter before he was halfway up the path from the barn. Grace and Ben and Leo were playing in the yard and went running as soon as they saw him. Annie could hear them hollering about her letter clear in the house.

She'd like to throttle the three of them, going and blabbing her news that way. A body couldn't do anything right and proper with the likes of them around. That Ben was the worst. What he needed was a good lesson, and she'd be glad to give it to him. Annie snatched up the masher and started in on the potatoes.

"Them potatoes will be mashed to milk, Annie," Mom said. "For goodness sakes, there's more to get on the table than that."

"Yes, Mom," Annie said. Quickly she scooped the potatoes into a bowl. Dad would ask her about the letter as soon as he came in. He'd be tired and hungry; it might not set good with him. Mom had told her once not to ever ask a man for anything or give him news till he was fed and full.

Dad came in the kitchen door, the boys and Grace right behind. Dad was tall and knobby like a pine. Annie looked a lot like him, except she had bones and blades jutting out like a skinny heifer. Grace was the beauty and Mae was tiny, the way Mom had once been.

Dad removed his jacket and hung it on a peg by the

door. He turned around. His gaze swept the room and settled on Annie standing at the stove.

"I hear you got an invite from the teacher," he said.

Two

Y es, Miss Osborne sent me a letter," Annie said. She searched Dad's face, but in the shadowy light she couldn't tell what he was thinking. "After supper I'll get it out so you can read it for yourself."

Dad nodded agreeably. He stooped down and lifted Grace's chin. "I'll sit you on my lap soon as I get cleaned up." He walked to the pantry, Grace skipping after him. Ben and Leo and Russell had washed and were waiting at the table. The boys were always ready to eat.

"I could use a hand with this old hen," Mom said. She lifted the corner of her apron and wiped the sweat from her face.

"Oh." Annie stared down at the dish of carrots in her hand. She'd been so intent on what Dad might be thinking. . . . She set the dish on the warming shelf and picked up the meat platter.

Mom had killed the hen just that morning. "I have a hankering for a good mess of chicken and biscuits," Mom had said, "and that old bird wasn't laying eggs no more." She had taken the hen to the woodshed and whacked its head off with a hatchet on the chopping block. Ben and Leo had poked sticks at the headless bird as it flew up and flopped back down in the wood chips.

"Hold the platter closer, Annie," Mom said. She stuck two forks into the hen and lifted it from the kettle onto the platter.

Annie set the platter by Dad's place; he always liked to do the carving.

No one talked much during the meal. Leo and Ben were already holding out their plates and begging Mom for pie by the time Annie began to eat. Those boys were such hogs. They ate like they hadn't had a crumb all day. She shook her head. A day's work gone . . . swallowed up whole. When she was grown up, things would be different.

Dad pushed back his plate. "I'll have a look at that letter now, Annie," he said.

Annie rose from her place and fetched Dad's eyeglasses from the windowsill where he kept them before she gave him the letter.

Annie watched Dad's face as he read. He looked up, puzzled. "What do you think she's inviting you for?"

Annie shook her head. "I don't know, Dad," she said.

Dad removed his eyeglasses and handed the letter back to Annie. "It's a bit odd, her asking you over, but

I don't see any harm in your going. Would you like to go?"

Would she like to go? Annie almost choked on her bite of food. "Yes, Dad, please. I would like to go." Her voice quivered only a little.

"There's Saturday's chores all the same," Mom said. She handed Dad's plate back to him with the largest slice of pie on it.

"Might be nice for Annie to go. Ben and Leo can help out with her chores," Dad said.

"Me, too. I can help Annie," Grace said, her mouth full of pie.

Annie was glad that Ben and Leo had left the table. Ben would have set up a howl and probably wrecked her chances of going.

"Just don't let her put any foolish notions in your head. We don't know her folks . . . might be strange."

"Yes, Dad," Annie said.

"And don't go getting any spinsterish ways from her," Russell said, staring into her face.

Annie looked away. Russell never said much, but when he did, it was as if he put a finger into her soul and pulled out something like Little Jack Horner did with his Christmas pie.

"I won't let her influence me. I have a mind of my own, Russell," Annie said, her chest getting hot with anger. "I might even teach her a thing or two."

"Now don't go being disrespectful to the teacher, Annie," Mom said, her face puckered with worry.

Dad laughed and picked his pie off his plate. "Annie's been reared proper, Esther. Miss Osborne could probably use some of Annie's sense." Dad pushed the end of the pie into his mouth. "Good pie, Esther."

Mom sat back looking pleased. Annie got up and started clearing the table. Well, now that it was decided, what would she wear? And what about the other eighth grade girls, Justine and Aletha? Had Miss Osborne invited them, too? It was a selfish thought, but she hoped the teacher hadn't asked the other girls.

"Could I take a lamp up to bed tonight, Mom?" she asked. She scraped the chicken bones from the plates into the empty pie tin.

"A lamp on Saturday night?" Dad asked. "What for?" Dad frowned on wasting good kerosene.

"I need to write a poem for school," Annie said. "I worked on it last night, but I didn't get it done." It seemed there was never enough time left for schoolwork after chores were done. At least in her room she could study without being pestered by the boys. Annie sighed. Maybe, if she was very lucky, Grace would be asleep.

Mom nodded. "That'd be all right, Warner," she said. "I'll take the lamp up when I put Grace to bed."

"Don't worry about the dishes, Mom," Annie said. "I can manage them by myself." She was grateful to Mom for taking her part. It was hard to tell about Mom; she was often moody.

"The *Grit* came today, Warner," Mom said. "Why not rest yourself some and read it aloud while I mend? Leave the boys to bring in the wood. Russell will chop the kindling for morning."

Russell got up, took his jacket from the peg, and went outdoors. Annie was still collecting silverware from the table. She saw a look pass between Mom and Dad. She often caught them passing looks. She wasn't sure, but she supposed this time it had something to do with her letter.

Dad reached over and brushed a hand over Mom's arm. "Better wind the clock first," he said, getting up and going over to the mantel clock on the sideboard.

Annie took the last of the dishes into the pantry to wash. She could hear Dad's deep voice coming from the parlor as she scrubbed on the pots. How she loved the peaceful evenings with just the rise and fall of Dad's voice coming from the parlor.

When Annie went up to bed, she took a dipper filled with hot water from the tank on the stove. She hated washing up in cold water.

Good. Grace was asleep, curled on her side, her knees pulled up to her chin. It was such a luxury to have a light to wash by and warm water and Grace not chattering like a squirrel.

Annie slid cautiously into bed so as not to wake her sister and smoothed out the letter from Miss Osborne.

Grace's head popped up. "Annie," she whispered.

Annie groaned.

14

"You going to write a po-em now?"

"Soon."

"Annie, you know what?"

"Grace! I'm trying to read my letter."

Grace had an injured look.

Annie sighed. "Just this one thing, Grace, and then no more talking, understand?"

Grace edged closer and whispered, "Annie, you know what?"

"No, Grace, I don't know what."

Grace lay back against the pillow, a look of pure pleasure on her face. "Mom is going to get a baby."

"A baby? A baby?" Annie felt as if she'd been slapped. She leaned back against the headboard. How would Grace ever know such a thing? "Grace, Mom isn't getting a baby," she said.

Grace got up on her knees, her hands on her hips. "Yes. Uh-huh. She is so. Mom said so. I heard her," Grace said.

"Mom said so. Mom told you she was getting a baby?"

Grace looked all-important. "Dad. She told Dad. Mom said, 'I'm going to have another baby,' and she cried." Grace rolled her eyes. "She cried . . . like I cried when I fell and bit through my lip and it bled." Grace paused, seeming to consider this.

"So . . . so then what?"

"'Hush, you'll wake Grace.' Dad said that."

"What else, Grace?" Annie said impatiently.

"'Leastways you've got Annie to help out this time,'" Grace said, making her voice go deeper like Dad's. She stopped and tilted her head to one side. "How's Mom going to have a baby? I kept waiting and looking, and there's no baby. Annie. Annie?"

Annie grabbed Grace by both arms. "Grace, was that Mom and Dad's exact words? Are you sure?" Annie asked, shaking her.

Grace's lower lip quivered. "Let go. You're hurting me," she whimpered.

Annie dropped Grace's arms and pulled her close. "I'm sorry, Grace. I . . ." Annie broke off. Another baby? Please, Lord, Grace had to be wrong. But Grace wasn't one to make up stories.

"Aren't you going to write your po-em, Annie?"

"Tomorrow. I'll have to do it tomorrow."

"Tomorrow's church day," Grace said, snuggling up closer to Annie in bed; the October nights soon chilled the upstairs. "Dad won't let you do schoolwork."

"I'll write a psalm instead," Annie said.

"A song?"

"A psalm. You know, like in the Bible. 'The Lord is my Shepherd, I shall not want.'"

"Can I write one, too, Annie?"

"If you keep quiet now and go to sleep." Grace, please be quiet, Annie thought. She had more important things to worry over than a poem.

Annie reached over and touched Grace's soft curls. She loved Grace so much, even when Grace pestered

16

her to death. But another baby? The thought was more than a body could bear.

THREE

A nnie! Annie!" Dad called up the stairs on Sunday morning.

Annie jerked awake and sprang from the bed. Why was Dad calling to her? Was something wrong?

"Annie!" he hollered, sharply this time.

Annie ran to the head of the stairs. "Dad, what's wrong? Is something wrong?" she said as she rubbed the sleep from her eyes. Dad had never called to her this way before.

"Your mom's ill. She's got to rest in bed this morning," he said, running his hands over the brim of his hat. He must have just come in from the morning milking, because he was still wearing his barn boots and jacket.

"Did you ring for the doctor?" Annie asked.

He shook his head. "No . . . no. Just come down and fix breakfast." He started away, then turned back. "Oh, you'll have to see to getting the boys and Grace to church."

"Yes, Dad," Annie said, feeling troubled. She hurried

18

back to her room to change and then rushed downstairs.

Annie chewed her lip as she sliced potatoes into the frying pan for breakfast. So, Grace was right. Mom was going to have a baby. "Leastways you've got Annie to help out this time," Dad had said. Wasn't she helping this very minute? Hadn't she always helped?

Later, after breakfast was cleared away, Annie helped Grace dress, and soon they were all hurrying out the door. The boys ran ahead; they were already out of sight by the time Annie and Grace got to the end of the driveway and started walking up the road.

"Annie, you're walking too fast!" Grace hollered, after they had gone around the bend past the Haineses' house. "I can't keep up."

"Sorry, Grace," Annie said and shortened her steps. She'd been thinking about Mom being sick and having another baby. It seemed as if there was never time for anything but chores, and from now on it would be even worse. Sometimes she wished she could run off somewhere and read a book straight through from beginning to end without having to stop to help with supper or dishes or cleaning and filling the lamps or emptying the chamber pots or . . .

"Annie, Annie, you've got to help us!" Ben called out. He and Leo came crashing out of the weeds and underbrush along the road.

"Just look at you two," Annie said. Their knickers and stockings were puckered with burdocks.

"Come on, help us pick them off," Leo said. "Please, Annie."

Annie's fingers shook as she worked at getting the stubborn burrs off the back of their stockings. "Can't you two ever stay out of mischief?"

"Come on, hurry up, Annie," Ben said.

"I *am* hurrying," Annie said.

"Can I go by myself?" Grace asked.

"You can stay and help," Annie said.

"But the burrs hurt my fingers," Grace said.

"Baby," Ben said.

"Baby," Leo said.

"I'm not a baby. I'm five!"

"Baby, baby, baby."

"All of you just stop it," Annie said.

"I hear somebody coming," Leo said. "It's a Ford."

"Chevy!" Ben shouted. "Don't you know anything? Come on, Leo. Let's see if we can beat it." The two of them ran off up the road.

Annie shook her head. She was almost afraid to have them out of her sight. Someday they were likely to get into real trouble.

She and Grace had walked just a ways farther when the auto passed them. It was their minister, Reverend Owens. He didn't slow down when he passed them. He didn't even seem to notice her and Grace.

"He was in an almighty rush, Grace," Annie said. "Maybe we're late. Maybe we should hurry; you might get to play with Mary Hathaway before church starts."

And maybe she could talk to Miss Osborne and accept the luncheon invitation. Maybe she could find out if either of the other girls was invited, too.

"Come on, Annie," Grace said, pulling on her hand. When they walked into the churchyard, the bell started ringing for service. Ben and Leo and Jack Hathaway were playing, chasing each other, darting among the autos parked alongside the church. They paid no attention to the bell.

"Ben! Leo!" Annie called. "It's time for church."

Ben came running from between two autos. He stopped when he saw Annie and waggled his fingers in his ears. "Make me! Make me!" he cried, then laughed gustily.

Annie sprang forward and snatched his coat sleeve. "What ails you, Ben Lucas? Acting like a heathen? What would Mom think?"

"Aw, Annie," Ben said, trying to shrug free. "I was fooling. Come on, you can take a little fooling."

Annie nodded. "Well, behave now and get inside," she said.

After they were inside and she had gotten Grace and the boys settled down, Annie looked around the congregation. The service was just starting, and a lot of the regulars like Mom weren't there—the Potters and the Pruetts, and even the Haineses were absent. Annie was particularly sorry not to see Miss Osborne. She sighed. She liked it best when the church was full—that way she could daydream if she wanted to—

but today she'd have to keep the boys and Grace from whispering and squirming, and Mom would want a detailed account of Reverend Owens's sermon.

Reverend Owens was a tall, very thin man with graying hair. Annie often thought that a strong wind would whip him about like a stalk of hay. It always surprised her when he spoke—his voice was deep and clear and filled every corner of the church. Today he was preaching about the evils of the world—the speakeasies and bootlegging and the rampant use of the automobile as a house of prostitution by the young folk. Annie couldn't see what any of it had to do with her, but he did weave powerful stories of the sinful life.

When church was over, Annie grabbed Ben and Leo before they ran off and herded them and Grace out of the church.

"Sorry to see your mother didn't attend this morning. She would've enjoyed the sermon," Reverend Owens said as he shook Annie's hand at the door. "There's nothing wrong at home, is there?" he asked.

"Mom wasn't feeling well this morning. Dad said she needed some extra rest, Reverend."

"Tell your mother my prayers are with her," Reverend Owens said. "And how are things at school?"

"Very good, thank you, Reverend," Annie said slowly, studying his face.

"Come on, Annie," Grace said, dragging on her hand. Annie moved on down the steps. What a strange question. In all the years he had been the preacher, this was the first time he had asked her about school.

FOUR

onday morning Annie was in the pantry
packing the dinner pails for school. Grace
was hanging close to her side. "Can I walk
part way with you, Annie? You won't have to go slow
for me. I'll take big steps. Just as far as Haineses',
Annie, please? Please? Can I?"

"Ask Mom, Grace. If Mom doesn't mind, you can
go."

Grace scurried out to the kitchen, where Mom was
clearing up from breakfast. Mom seemed to be feeling
poorly this morning. She kept sitting down; her face
was white.

As Ben and Leo came into the pantry for their
dinner pails, Annie heard the kitchen door slam. Must
be Dad and Russell going out to the barn to finish the
morning chores.

"I'll bet you can't wait to tell the whole school Miss
Osborne sent you a letter," Ben said with a sneer.

Annie's back prickled with anger. It was the last
thing she had in mind. She turned around slowly. "Now,
Ben, why would I go saying anything? I figured you

would just do the telling for me," she said sweetly. She handed him and Leo their dinner pails. "Why don't you hurry ahead now and do that?"

Ben's mouth dropped open. Leo snorted with laughter. "Come on, Leo," Ben said crossly. He elbowed his brother and scowled. "It ain't funny," he said.

Annie smiled and watched as they disappeared through the doorway of the pantry. Ben would never tell now. She picked up her pail and went to the kitchen and hung her pinafore on one of the pegs by the door.

"Mom said I can go. I can go, Annie. Get my coat. Can I carry your reader? I won't drop it. Please, Annie?" Grace asked as Annie helped her with her coat.

Annie bit her lip and picked up her reader. She hated having anyone touch her schoolbooks, least of all her reader. Maybe Grace would try to be careful, but she would start chattering and probably drop the book. Annie couldn't bear the thought of "Evangeline" or "Hiawatha" having bent pages or finger marks or dirt stains. "Grace," she said, holding her reader tight against her chest, "if you want to go, I'll let you carry my dinner pail."

"You never let me carry your reader," Grace said, picking up Annie's pail. "I wish I could go to school. I can write my name. Why can't I go?"

"Shh." Annie put a finger on Grace's lips. "Be a big girl, now." Annie smoothed the curls back from Grace's eyes. "And don't talk so much. Justine likes to do the talking."

"Will Justine holler at me like last time?" Grace asked as they went out the kitchen door.

"If you talk too much, she will," Annie said, starting down the driveway.

"How much is too much?" Grace asked.

"Shh, just be quiet," Annie whispered.

Justine and Aletha were waiting at the mailbox. Justine was wearing a new dress. She was the only girl Annie knew who wore dresses that had been bought in a store.

Mom made almost all of their clothes, except Dad's and the boys' overalls, which were ordered through the Sears & Roebuck catalog. Mom was fussy with her sewing, and her dresses were always nice, but there was something different about clothes bought in a store . . . something that made a person better somehow. She wouldn't want Justine to know it, but when her friend talked about shopping and dining in town, Annie hung on every word. It was important to know the proper way to act, because someday she planned to live in town.

Justine looked perturbed. "Is *she* coming again?"

"Annie said I could. As far as the Haineses'. Didn't you, Annie? Annie said. . . ."

"Grace." Annie gripped Grace's hand tighter in warning. "Your new dress looks real pretty, Justine," Annie said quickly. She fell into step beside Aletha as they started walking up the dirt road.

Aletha was her cousin on Dad's side. She was also half-Native American. Dad remarked at times how Aletha's dad could walk through the woods without making a sound. Aletha was pretty soundless, too.

Justine cleared her throat. "Like I was saying to Aletha, Mother and Father and I left early on Saturday for Bradford, soon after it was light. I wore my best . . . you know, the green velvet with the ocher-colored lace on the bodice. Father had some important business, and Mother and I shopped for new dresses. We dined at the Hotel Algonquin and sat right under a beautiful chandelier. It was made all of glass . . . glass beads . . . glass prisms. It shimmered and sparkled." Justine drew in her breath. "I wish we lived in Bradford. When I'm grown up, I'm going to live in a city or at least a big town like Bradford where there are electric lights and indoor plumbing and stores filled with beautiful dresses. I hate outhouses and kerosene lamps and cows everywhere."

"We're at the Haineses' now, Grace. You'd better get back. Mom will worry," Annie said.

Grace looked crestfallen. "But I didn't get to hear you tell about the teacher's letter."

Oh, Grace. How could you? Annie thought. She bent over and swiped the dinner pail from Grace's hand. "March home right now, young lady, or I won't let you walk with me ever again," she whispered.

Grace's lip trembled, but she turned for home.

"What did Grace mean, Annie?" Justine scowled. "Annie?"

Annie shrugged. "Miss Osborne invited me to have luncheon with her on Saturday."

"She invited *you*. . . . Why?" Justine's face turned red.

Annie shook her head. "I don't know."

"Are your ma and pa letting you go?" Justine asked.

"Dad said I might."

Justine pressed her lips together and walked the rest of the way with her head bent. When the girls got to the school, Leo was standing in the doorway clanging the bell for everyone to come in. The bell seemed almost as big as Leo, who was small for his age. Ben, just eighteen months older and only a third grader, was sturdy and already a head taller than Leo. Ben was the leader among the younger boys at school.

Annie hurried inside ahead of the other girls. Miss Osborne sat quietly at her desk, her back straight as she looked out at the schoolroom. The teacher was tiny like Mae, yet her dark hair and clothes seemed to blend in with the very darkness of her desk in a strong, immovable way. With halting steps, Annie approached her teacher. "Morning, Miss Osborne. Thank you for the invitation. My folks said I could go," she said in a rush.

"Why, you're welcome, Annie. I'm so pleased that you'll be coming," Miss Osborne said, giving her a warm smile.

Annie smiled back and then hurried to her seat in the row behind the wood stove. Saturday seemed so far away. Annie sighed and opened her composition book and read over her poem. It was only one stanza. She had wanted to write more about the ocean, but the only other thing she knew to write was that the ocean had salt in it. It seemed peculiar that water could be salty. Mom made her gargle with salt water when she had a sore throat, but Mom put the salt in. . . . Annie closed her book. The poem would have to do.

When the morning chores had been assigned and taken care of and the Pledge and Lord's Prayer were over, Miss Osborne stood and walked around to the front of her desk. "Today is going to be different; today we are going to use our imaginations. We are going to explore within ourselves."

Miss Osborne whirled around. Her dark blue dress rustled as she strode to the blackboard. She yanked on the map of the world. "This is where we are!" She took up her pointer and stabbed at New York State. Miss Osborne shook her head. "But the world is ours for the taking. . . . See, it is at our fingertips." She spread her hands and rested them on the hemispheres. Some boy in the back of the room snickered. Most likely it was Ben.

Miss Osborne sucked in her breath and turned slowly around. "Justine, dear, would you collect the composition books? Let's discover how many pupils were able to explore themselves in poetry."

Miss Osborne sorted through the notebooks that Justine had placed on her desk. She picked out one and leafed through it. Her gaze rested for a moment on Annie. The teacher began to speak:

"Let's stroll along by the ocean,
by the white and sandy beach.
Let's take off our shoes and stockings,
and wade in the ocean deep.

"This is a wonderful poem—it expresses the beginnings of a wish, a desire. This poet has begun an exploration." Miss Osborne slowly closed Annie's book. "The ocean . . . has anyone ever been to the ocean?" she asked.

But no one had, not even Justine.

Miss Osborne stroked her cheek. She looked thoughtful as she set Annie's book aside and smiled slightly to herself. "Well, let's share a few more poems," she said, leafing through several other notebooks. "Hmm . . . it seems that many of you missed the idea of expressing a desire, but perhaps we can remedy that later on today." Miss Osborne smiled in a secret, mysterious way. "But for now we will continue with our usual morning work. Will my first readers come to the recitation bench, please?"

When it was time for recess, and everyone was rushing out, Miss Osborne drew Annie aside. "There's something I need to get from home. I hope to be back before recess is over, but if I'm not, perhaps you can read something to occupy the children for a while."

Annie wet her lips. "Nothing's wrong? You aren't ill?"

"No, no," Miss Osborne said with a laugh. "I couldn't be better." She paused and smiled warmly. "Now don't worry. It's a surprise—your poem gave me a marvelous idea," she said. "I'd better run along so I can get back. Come on, walk out with me."

Annie waved to Miss Osborne as she drove away. What could the surprise be? And to think that her poem had given the teacher a *marvelous* idea! Annie tingled with excitement. She hurried back into the schoolhouse. If the teacher wasn't back when recess was over, what should she read?

There was a small shelf of books in the back corner, next to the pail of drinking water. Annie picked out *Treasure Island*. It was Ben's favorite.

When recess was over, the teacher was still not back. "Where's the teacher? Where is she?" everyone demanded of Annie when they crowded back into the room.

Annie walked to Miss Osborne's desk and rapped on the edge with a ruler. "Everyone, please take your seat," she said. "The teacher had to go home. She'll be back shortly." She saw Ben's look of defiance, as if daring her to make him do what *she* said. Annie grinned at him. "I'm going to read from *Treasure Island.*"

"Hurry up to your seats," Ben said, pushing past Leo and Wilfred.

Annie sat down in Miss Osborne's chair and opened the book. "'Fifteen men on a dead man's chest—'" Annie paused and looked back at Ben. He jumped to his feet and hollered out, "'Yo-ho-ho, and a bottle of rum!'"

Just at the end of chapter two, Miss Osborne rushed in. "Thank you, Annie," she said. She was out of breath and carrying a wooden box. The teacher put the box down on her desk and then stood back, her hands on her hips. "Well," she said, "I've brought you the ocean."

Everyone stared at the mysterious box, but Miss Osborne paced back and forth, clasping and unclasping her hands.

"One summer," she began, "my parents and I traveled by train to the seashore along the Carolina coast. That's on the Atlantic Ocean." She stopped and pointed to it on the map.

"The seashore is different from anything I have ever seen. The land is flat, the climate is quite hot, and the ocean water is pleasantly warm and salty, with all kinds of creatures in it. Many of the creatures live in seashells. They are similar to snails or crayfish, but their shells are often colorful, and some are quite large.

"There are birds, sea gulls, that circle and cry and

dive for fish, but sometimes they just sit in the water like ducks." She tried to mimic the sound of the gulls. "I sound more like a crow," she said, laughing.

Ben raised his hand. "If it's called the ocean, Miss Osborne, why ain't . . . isn't it ocean gulls and ocean shells and ocean shore?"

Miss Osborne laughed. "That's a very good question, Ben, but I don't know." She stepped up to the box then and lifted out a large shell. "This is a conch," she said. "It's spelled c-o-n-c-h. It has a special magic. If you hold it to your ear like this," she said, showing them, "you will hear the waves of the ocean." She walked over to the first row and handed the shell to Mary Hathaway.

Annie watched as the shell made its way around the room. At last she held the shell in her own hands and placed it against her ear. It was true. She could hear the ocean, the waves rolling over each other, lapping against the shore.

Annie closed her eyes. A desire to see the ocean welled up inside. It was a mystery, a miracle, a story-book place like *Treasure Island*. . . .

"Hurry up with that." Albert Potter nudged her arm. "I ain't heard the ocean yet."

Reluctantly, Annie passed him the shell. But now Miss Osborne had taken out a wooden bowl filled with sand. "I'm going to pass around this bowl. I want you to pick up a handful of the sand. Imagine that it is hot, almost too hot to hold. That's the way the sand on the shore would be in the summer."

When the bowl came to Annie, she buried her fingers in the sand. She scooped up a handful and let it sift slowly through her fingers. It was dazzling white—so clean. Again she closed her eyes. She imagined gulls crying overhead, the sun golden and blazing, the sound of the ocean waves, the sand pressing up between her toes and hot on the soles of her feet. She sighed. Seemed like New York State was never warm enough. The winters were so long and dreadfully cold.

Albert nudged her again. "Annie, stop being such a big hog. I want a turn!"

Miss Osborne was taking shells of all shapes and sizes out of the box and spreading them on top of her desk. "Please, everyone, come up and look at the shells."

While the children stood around her desk and studied the shells, Miss Osborne picked up a piece of chalk and wrote Annie's poem on the blackboard. "I think we have had a wonderful morning at the ocean," she said.

Annie thought it was the best school day she could ever remember, but it only made her longing to leave home press harder on her heart.

FIVE

W hen Annie stepped inside the kitchen after school that day, her sister Mae was flitting about the room. She was laughing and pulling candies from a little bag and giving them to Grace.

"Mae!" Annie cried, her voice breaking. The last time Mae had gotten home was for the Fourth of July in the summer.

"Come give your sister a hug," Mae said, coming up and hugging her before Annie had a chance to move. Mae was so dainty, so sure of herself. Annie was at once conscious of her own sturdy tallness.

"But how did you get here? How long can you stay?" Annie asked.

Mom looked up wearily from the cookstove. "I could use a hand getting supper on the table," she said stiffly. "There's time for chitchat at the table. The boys and Dad will be coming in from the barn any second now."

"Yes, Mom," Annie murmured. She put her books on the sideboard and took her pinafore from its peg and hung her coat in its place.

Mae sat at the table watching as Annie put the plates on. Grace leaned against Mae and chewed happily on a stick of licorice.

"Mama says you're going to the teacher's for a luncheon come Saturday. That right?"

Annie nodded.

"What you going to wear, hmmm? Maybe I got something in my valise to fix you up a bit. After supper . . ."

Mom turned quickly and gave Mae a dark look.

"Now, Mama, I'm not meaning to put any powder or lipstick on her."

Mae followed Annie out to the pantry. "After supper . . . oh, Annie, have I got lots to tell you." Mae rolled her eyes. "I'm spending the night; the shirt factory closed down for two whole days. My friend Gladys, you know, the girl I share a room with at the boarding house—her aunt drove us out. Dropped me right off at the front step."

Some of Mae's gayness began to rub off on her. "Did you happen to bring any magazines?" Annie asked, her voice low so Mom wouldn't hear. Mom didn't approve of worldly things, and it seemed as if everything about town was worldly to Mom.

Ben and Leo rushed into the pantry then to wash up for supper. Dad's and Russell's voices could be heard in the kitchen.

Annie scooped up the silverware and hurried out to help Mom. "Bring the glasses, Mae," she called.

When supper was spread and the boys were hungrily plowing through the food, Mae, who was still carefully cutting her meat, spoke up. "I was just saying to my Elmer the other day, 'Why, Elmer,' I said, 'what would I do without you?' I declare, Mama, it isn't one bit safe these days for a young lady to walk the streets in town alone. Why, just the other day—in broad daylight—robbers held up the bank. They had guns." Mae paused, letting this information sink into everyone's head. "And one of them was a woman, Mama." Mae rolled her eyes heavenward. "And the bootlegging that's going on—something fierce," she said, wagging her head and clucking her tongue. Mae sighed. "I just don't know what I would do without my Elmer."

Annie looked around the table. They were all so taken up with eating that no one seemed to mind what Mae was saying, except Mom. Mom sat stiff-faced and staring at the wall. She was praying. Annie knew it. Praying her children would be delivered from such evil and wickedness as there was in the world . . . as there was in town. Why did Mae have to say such things? Mom would never let a single blessed one of them leave home, if Mae didn't stop her carrying on.

"Now, Mae," Russell said, "I'd be one to think you'd put your trust in the Lord, not Elmer."

Mae's face turned rose-colored. She stared down at her plate.

"Well, Mae," Dad said, "I think we're all mighty glad you've got a young man to look out for you."

"Thanks, Dad," Mae said, smiling over at him.

Mom shook her head. "Still, the Good Book says the Lord will take care of his own, Mae," Mom said reprovingly. "You need to rely on the Lord. You cannot serve God and Mammon."

* * *

"Oh, Annie, Annie," Mae said, when Annie came into the bedroom later, after the dishes were done up. Mae had sweetened up Mom and talked her into having Grace sleep downstairs. Mae seemed to know how to get her own way.

Mae stood in front of the bureau mirror and stripped off her clothes.

Annie didn't know where to look. It didn't seem proper for a woman of twenty to undress in front of her that way. Mae proceeded to wash and admire herself. The chilliness didn't seem to bother her.

"How can you stand this backward life, Annie?" Mae said with a huge sigh. "I thank my lucky stars every day that I am out of here. It's been five years since I ran away. Mama never has forgiven me, has she? See the way she carried on at dinner? Nothing would make her happier than for me to marry some poor farmer and live just down the road apiece. I've never been sorry for that time I went off to town with Gladys, knowing she and I was getting jobs at the factory. Annie, sometimes you just got to take matters into your hands, make your own choices and not go waiting around for other people to have all the say-so about your life. Well . . . enough of that. Hand me my bag, would you? That's a dear." Mae undid the clasp and took out a pile of magazines. She flung them onto the bed—*True Story, Modern Screen, The Saturday Evening Post.*

"The girls from the factory pitched in. I told them what a reader you are. Gladys sent a hammock novel . . . a real spicy romance," Mae said, winking and switching her hips. "But you take care with that book; she wants it back." Mae patted herself dry and dropped her nightgown over her head.

"Well, now," Mae said, hoisting herself up on the bed and lying back against the pillows. "You'll have plenty to read when I've left."

Annie stared hungrily at the magazines. It was an effort not to grab them up. Heavens, she could just lock herself in the outhouse for a week.

"Wait till you hear, Annie. You'll turn pure green with envy, I swear. Annie, are you paying attention?" Mae raised up off the pillow and made sure Annie was hanging on her every word. "Annie, me and Elmer are getting married. He asked me right after service this past Sunday," she whispered deliciously, her eyes getting wide. "First chance he gets, he's coming out to ask Mama and Daddy for my hand. It's just so far to come—pretty near fifty miles—and he's so busy with his automobile business, but he's teaching me to drive, Annie. Elmer says I'm a natural. One of these days, I'm going to surprise you and come motoring up all on my own. You mustn't say a word about any of this. You won't, will you? Promise me?"

Annie nodded and hunkered down against the foot railing to make herself seem smaller.

"Isn't that just the best? Elmer's looking for a little place for just the two of us. Elmer's so sweet. He'd do just about anything for me. Soon as he finds a house, we're getting married. Oh, Annie, I can't wait. You can come for a little visit sometime."

"Maybe I could stay with you some . . . when I'm finished with school. I'd get a job. I wouldn't be any bother, Mae," Annie blurted out.

Mae's eyes glittered. She sat up. "What made you ask that? You're much too young to leave home." Mae slid to the floor. She went to the bureau and pulled the pins from her hair. The curls fell softly about her shoulders. "Gracious me, Annie, how can you stand the smell of yourself?" Mae shuffled through her valise and pulled out a tin of talcum. "I'll just leave my talcum for you. Wouldn't hurt if you used some this very minute," she said and laughed. Her voice tinkled like empty perfume bottles clinking together, and she wrinkled her nose.

Annie stared at the tin of powder being thrust toward her, and she shook her head.

"Well, take it now," Mae said, advancing toward her.

Annie turned her face away and hugged the iron foot railing. What was Mae thinking? She was so warm one minute, and so . . . so worldly the next. Did Mae actually expect her to undress, right there in front of her? What would Mom think of such a thing?

Mae dropped the tin on Annie's lap and proceeded to climb into bed.

Six

At last it was Saturday. At last Annie would be going to Miss Osborne's. She rushed through scrubbing the outhouse as soon as the breakfast dishes were done and the beds made. The night before, Annie had laid out her clothes—her best set of everything and her best dress—the white muslin Mom had made her before canning season in the summer. Mom had embroidered dainty violets on the yoke. Mae had left her a violet ribbon to match.

Mom and Mae could embroider and crochet finer than anyone. Annie did a fair job, but mostly she didn't have the patience for it. She'd never be a real lady.

Usually Annie didn't mind wearing her brown shoes, but now that she was dressed up, with a ribbon tied in her hair, the brown shoes seemed boyish and shabby. Annie chewed her lip. There was nothing she could do about it. They were her only pair. At least she was walking over, and it was a warm day, warm as August. She couldn't very well wear fancy shoes for walking on a dusty road.

Annie stood for a moment in front of the bureau mirror before going downstairs. She'd probably never be pretty the way Mae was, but she was satisfied with just looking good.

When she was about to leave, Mom suddenly began to fret about manners. "Make sure you say please and thank you, and don't pick onions out of your food. If there is onions in anything, promise me you won't pick them out. And don't scrape leftover butter off your knife back onto the dish, and don't hunch over." Mom drew a long breath, her face still puckered with worry. "You might as well use a splash of my toilet water, if you want. It'd be a shame to go off all dressed so pretty without a dab of something," she said. She gave Annie one of her best hankies to tuck in her belt and a jar of elderberry jelly for Miss Osborne.

Mom and Grace stood on the porch steps to see her off; Leo and Ben sulked in the background. Annie had promised Ben she would bring home *Treasure Island* and read it all the way through to make up to him for helping with her chores. Ben had sniffed and said he guessed that'd be all right. Grace clung to her and cried, heartbroken that Annie was going off without her. Grace was still waving when Annie got to the bridge and looked back at the house one last time.

Then finally she was out of sight of the house, and her heart thudded. She was really on her way. It seemed a wild, carefree adventure to go off alone, away from the comfort of everyday life, for who knew what? Miss Osborne surely had something in mind. The sun was bright, the leaves were golden and burnt orange, the sky was blue, and she was a young lady going off to a proper luncheon. It was better than dining in Bradford on any day.

It wasn't until she was in view of the creamery that the day seemed to be less bright. Justine's dad owned the creamery, and their house was right across the road from it. What if Justine saw her, dressed in old shoes and a pretty dress? And there'd be men coming to the creamery to drop off milk cans. There were some that might holler out or whistle.

Annie stopped still in the road and considered, then cut across the Hathaways' field and up over the hillside through the woods.

When Annie came out of the woods by the abandoned Lester place, she heard water gurgling. She had forgotten about the brook that ran down along the edge of the woods. In the summer, when she and Mom went berrying, the streambed was dry, but with the fall rains and near floods, it had come to life. She couldn't risk leaping across; the bank was too steep. She'd have to wade.

"You'll catch your death of cold," Mom would have scolded fiercely, but no one was around to see. Annie unlaced her shoes and undid her garters and rolled her cotton stockings down around her ankles and tugged them off. She tucked them carefully into her shoes, then pulled her dress up around her buttocks and knotted the material in front. The knot would wrinkle the muslin something awful, but it couldn't be helped. She scooped up her shoes and the jelly and stepped gingerly into the water.

The frosty nights had made the water chilly; it sent shoots of pain up her legs. It'd take only a minute to cross the stream, but it'd take her the rest of the day to warm up again. Suddenly her summer dress seemed much too thin, and even with the brightness of the sun, her skin prickled with goose bumps.

But she was soon on the opposite bank and struggling to pull her stockings back on. She managed at last to fasten them, but now they lay plastered in wrinkles to her wet legs. She looked, she decided, as if she'd slept in her clothes. What would the teacher think?

She glanced across the field, spotted the Perry place where Miss Osborne boarded, and started off again. If only she had stayed on the road, her dress would look freshly ironed and her stockings would be dry and neat. She could have looked a proper lady.

Just as Annie was halfway across the field, she saw a dark speck and a cloud of red shale dust stirring up against the blue sky at the top of the hill. Someone was coming with a horse and wagon. She pressed the jar of elderberry jelly against her chest and ran through the tall brown weeds. If she hurried, she could cross the road and get to the Perrys' drive without getting caught in the clouds of dust. The driver must have seen her running, because the horse was reined to a halt a ways up the hill from her. She stopped at the edge of the road.

"Go on, cross over," the young driver hollered.

"Thank you," she called, briefly waving a hand as she started across the road. He inched the horse forward slowly and came almost alongside as she got to the Perrys' drive. He lifted his cap and grinned. "And good day to you."

He looked about sixteen, Annie thought. She remembered seeing him once with his family at a box social two summers ago. Dad had pointed him out, said they were well-to-do farmers, but Annie couldn't remember their name.

She nodded back to him and quickly turned away. She straightened her shoulders and forced herself to walk, even though she could tell he was watching her, maybe even smirking at her.

When Annie walked around the bend in the drive, she could see Miss Osborne sitting in a rocking chair on the porch. Miss Osborne waved when she saw Annie and came out to meet her.

If the teacher noticed the wrinkles in Annie's dress, she didn't let on. "Isn't it a simply gorgeous day?" Miss Osborne said. "Why, Annie, what lovely flowers on your dress!" she exclaimed.

Annie shifted her eyes away from the teacher's face. "Mom did that, and she sent you this." Annie thrust the jar of jelly at Miss Osborne. "It's elderberry."

Miss Osborne took the jar. "Be sure to thank your mom for me. I've heard she makes the best jelly around." Miss Osborne linked an arm with Annie and drew her toward the house.

Annie knew then that her brown shoes didn't matter. She could have worn an everyday dress; it wouldn't have mattered at all to the teacher.

"We have the house to ourselves," Miss Osborne said, opening the screen. "The Perrys have gone to visit Mrs. Perry's sister in Little Eddy for a few days."

They went inside, and Miss Osborne set the jelly down on the kitchen table. "I hope you're hungry. Or, maybe, I hope you're not hungry. I made a big pot of stew. I've never done much cooking," she confessed, all in a rush. "Mother always had a cook, and now Mrs. Perry makes my meals. I just never learned."

Annie was surprised to see her teacher blushing and surprised, too, that Miss Osborne seemed, well, not like a teacher, but just an ordinary person.

"It smells good," Annie said.

"Could you, I mean, would you know how much longer it might take for the stew to cook? I can't tell," Miss Osborne said, lifting the lid on the pot.

Annie went over and peered in. She fought back an urge to laugh. The potatoes and carrots and onions were peeled, but whole, and the water was just coming to a simmer.

"What do you think?" Miss Osborne asked.

How could she tell the teacher that the stew wouldn't be ready until supper? "I think . . . I think . . ." Annie slid her eyes toward Miss Osborne. Why did she have to look so anxious? "It's, well, it's not going to be done for a while," she said slowly. Dad had been right. There probably were a lot of things she could teach Miss Osborne. "Why don't we start with tea," Annie suggested. It seemed she had come just for a luncheon after all and not for any special reason. Perhaps Miss Osborne just wanted some company.

"But, Annie, how much longer is a while?" Miss Osborne asked, looking worried. She put the lid back.

"Well . . . you'd best plan on it for supper," Annie said, moving away from the stove.

"I knew I shouldn't try making anything," Miss Osborne said, folding her arms over her chest and giving the pot a dark look. "It's a good thing for us that Mrs. Perry made fresh bread yesterday." She turned toward Annie, her cheeks flaming red. "Oh, and there's your mom's jelly," she said, clapping her hands together the way Grace might. "I know, we'll have a tea party instead."

When they were settled at the table with their cups of tea and jelly and bread, Miss Osborne spoke. "You've probably been wondering why I asked you to lunch?"

Annie nodded. Lord, had she wondered anything but?

Miss Osborne sipped her tea. "Annie, have you ever given any consideration to attending high school?"

"High school? No . . ." Annie shook her head. There was never any reason to think of high school. No one she knew, except for the teachers and the Reverend, had ever been to high school.

"If you had a choice . . . I mean, if you could go to high school, would you want to?"

"Yes," Annie blurted out. "Oh, yes!"

"Good. I think you should go to high school. You have a great deal of potential and a natural ability to teach as well as learn. It would be a shame to waste it. I want you to go. I will help you. My parents will help you. I've already spoken to them about it. They would love to have you come and stay with them and go on to school."

Annie was stunned. Her head was light with excitement. Leave home at fourteen? Go to high school? She could become a teacher. "Why, it would be wonderful."

Miss Osborne clasped her hands together. "I just knew you would love my idea. But we have work to do. You'll have to take the entrance exams . . . and your folks—of course they'll let you go?"

Her folks? Mom and Dad? Annie stared at her half-eaten slice of bread and jelly. "Leastways you've got Annie to help out this time," Dad had said.

Annie looked up slowly and swallowed. "I think we'd best wait a bit to ask my folks."

SEVEN

nnie, you can't mean that your parents wouldn't want you to go to high school?" Miss Osborne asked, looking surprised. "But surely . . ."

Annie shook her head and stared down at her plate. "Mom's having another baby, for one thing, and they'll be wanting me to help out more," she said.

Annie looked across at Miss Osborne. "And . . . and, well, it . . . it wouldn't matter to Mom and Dad if I go or not." She couldn't explain better than that. It was something she just knew, not anything Mom or Dad had said. Going to high school was something people like them never thought of to even worry over. "I suppose everybody in town goes to high school," Annie said.

"Many do," Miss Osborne said, setting down her empty teacup. "But there's plenty that don't finish for one reason or another."

Annie found it comforting that not the whole world outside of South Branch knew more than she.

Miss Osborne sighed. "Well, Annie, I think all it will

take is for me to discuss this with your parents. Surely when they realize what potential you have . . ."

Annie shook her head. "No, please . . . not yet. I need to talk to them first, get them thinking on it. . . ."

"I see." Miss Osborne bit her lip and looked down. "Well . . . then that settles it for now," she said with a sigh.

"But I'll talk to them real soon," Annie said quickly.

Miss Osborne looked at her and smiled. "Things will work out for you, Annie. You'll see," she said, pushing back her chair. "I nearly forgot—there's something I've been wanting to show you." She jumped to her feet and hurried from the room but was back in an instant with a photograph album. She came around the table and pulled a chair over next to Annie. "Ever since you wrote that lovely poem about the seashore, and we had such fun with the shells and all, I've wanted to show this to you."

Miss Osborne opened the cover of the album. "There are some of the photographs taken at the seashore. Look, there's me in my bathing suit. Mama insisted I carry a sunshade so I wouldn't freckle." Miss Osborne laughed. "Oh, no, here's Papa and me building a sand castle."

Annie leaned closer and studied the photograph. Miss Osborne and her father were sitting on the beach. Their arms were covered with sand and, sure enough, a castle was rising out of the sand. Annie stared in wonder. A grown man and a schoolteacher playing like youngsters? She laughed. Imagine Dad doing such a thing . . . or even her.

Miss Osborne's gaiety faded suddenly. "My parents want me to stop teaching here after this year and come back home. They say I should continue my education so I can get a better teaching position." She sighed and dropped her hands down into her lap. "I can't decide. I love teaching here so much, but I miss my parents and my friends. Annie, I do get lonely at times," she said, getting quiet and very still.

Annie couldn't think of two words to put together. Miss Osborne wasn't acting at all like a teacher. "I want to be a teacher—the same as you," she blurted out, feeling overcome with some powerful emotion that the preacher might warn of from the pulpit.

Miss Osborne reached over and clasped Annie's hand. "You will. Somehow, you must."

Annie gazed out through the window and was troubled to see how long the shadows had become. The afternoon had gone so swiftly; the Perrys' kitchen was already losing its lazy warmth. "It's late," Annie said, pushing back her chair. "I'll do up the dishes, then I'd best get home."

"Don't worry about these few lunch things," Miss Osborne said. "Your mother will be getting concerned. You must let me drive you over. It gets so chilly these days even before the sun sets."

It wouldn't be dark for a few hours yet, but Annie didn't argue. Mom would want her home. There was

52

always plenty to do and extra food to get ready for Sunday. But it was so peaceful here with just the sound of their voices and the stew simmering on the stove. She could just sink into the quiet and dream about going off to high school . . . dream about becoming a teacher like Miss Osborne.

Annie's dizzy excitement over the teacher's talk of high school faded as they bumped along the road to the house. A heaviness spread through her.

She didn't want to go home. She wanted the pleasant, uncluttered visit with Miss Osborne to go on and on. For a while, at least, she had felt a bit special, like a lady even, and not just someone to do chores.

When Miss Osborne pulled into the driveway, Grace and Ben and Leo were hanging onto the porch post, but they bounded out, hooting and hollering as soon as the teacher stopped by the house. Grace's face was dirty and smeared with food.

How could Mom let them go about looking so ragged? Annie bit her lip and felt shamed over the way they were all acting so . . . so crude. Miss Osborne was such a fine lady.

"Thank you for the nice luncheon. I had a real nice time," Annie said. She stayed in the seat for a moment, not wanting the day to be over.

"It was a pleasant time for me, too, Annie," Miss Osborne said, taking her hand. "I'm anxious to get things settled so we can make definite plans. Annie, please speak to your parents soon."

"Hey, Miss Osborne!" Ben hollered. He jumped on the running board and stuck his head through her window.

"Ben!" Annie said, giving him a mean look.

Miss Osborne laughed. "How do, Ben," she said. "Want to go home with me? I'll let you check my school papers."

Ben jumped down, shaking his head. "No, ma'am. No schoolwork for me," he said.

Annie opened her door and stepped down off the running board. "Thank you!" she called as Miss Osborne backed away. Already the luncheon seemed long ago.

Ben and Leo and Grace ran toward the house hollering "Annie's home! Annie's home!"

Annie started slowly up to the porch. What ailed her, anyway? She should be happy. Hadn't the day been exciting? Didn't she have everything to look forward to? If only the here and now weren't so hard.

"Hey, Annie." Russell had come up behind her and made her jump. "Daydreaming?" he asked, grabbing her playfully by an arm and pulling her around to face him. "How was your luncheon?" He grinned and studied her face.

"Fine. It was fine," she said, turning her face away.

"Annie." He leaned close and whispered in her ear, "What did the lady schoolteacher want?"

"Why, nothing, nothing at all," she said, breaking free and scuttling into the house.

Mom was paring winter squash when Annie walked

into the kitchen. Ben and Leo were tearing about through the house.

If Russell hadn't been filling the doorway behind her, she would have backed out and fled. Lord, oh, Lord, who would ever choose this life?

Mom looked up. "Get your clothes changed and give me a hand with this squash. I've about had enough. Grace, would you stop that whining? Russell, would you take those two boys and find some chores at the barn for them? All they've done is caterwaul all afternoon." Mom burst into tears.

Russell pushed past Annie and went to her. He lifted the pan of squash from her lap and set it on the table. "You need a rest, Mom. Take a rest now. You fuss too much—work yourself near to death all the time." Russell took her hand and pulled her to her feet. "Come on now, Mom. Get your sweater and sit on the porch for a bit."

Mom was crying quietly now. "You're such a good son, Russell. Always worried about your mom," she said. "Heaven knows, those boys do get the better of me."

"Annie's here now. She'll finish the squash. Won't you, Annie?" Russell gave her a dark look as he steered Mom toward the door.

Annie filled up with fury. Those boys, Mom had said. Those boys? And now Mom was going and having another baby.

Annie stormed through the house and up the stairs

to her room and stripped off her good clothes. She pulled on an old dress and began buttoning it up.

"Annie?"

"What?" she said crossly.

Grace peeked around the door. "Can I come in?"

"I guess," she said.

Grace came in, clutching the reader Annie had brought her from school one day. "I waited and waited for you, Annie. Nobody would help me with my reader," Grace said, leaning against Annie's side.

"I have to finish cutting the squash for pies, Grace," Annie said. She bent over and hugged Grace for a minute. "Bring the reader downstairs. I'll help you while I work."

Down in the kitchen, Annie slipped on her pinafore and picked up the pan of squash. Grace pulled a chair over next to her and opened the reader. "Teach me this one, Annie," she said.

Annie picked up a piece of squash and looked over at the book. "'The sky is falling! The sky is falling! cried Chicken Licken,'" Annie read. *"The* is the first word, Grace. What are the letters in *the?"* Annie asked as she peeled the thick skin from the squash.

"T-h-e, *the,"* Grace said. "'The sky is falling,'" she said, moving her finger along under each word.

Annie tossed a chunk of squash into the pot and pressed her lips together. How could she ever talk to Mom or Dad about high school? They didn't understand. Dad would go along with whatever Mom said, and Mom was the problem. She was more changeable than the phases of the moon, and lately Mom's moods were all on the dark side. It appeared that it could be some time before Mom got her good temper back, and Annie had no choice but to wait.

Eight

Annie watched for an opportunity to talk to Mom about high school, but mornings Mom was ill and not able to stay on her feet long enough to cook breakfast, and evenings after supper there were extra chores because Mom couldn't keep up with the day's work.

"I'll be feeling better soon, Annie," Mom would say. "This ailment won't last much longer," Mom told her nearly every day. "I'm so thankful for your help. I don't know how I'd manage without you."

Some ailment! Some days Annie didn't blame Mae for running away. How else did a person escape the endless chores?

But one Friday early in November, Mom was up and busy cooking home fries and eggs for breakfast when Annie came downstairs.

"Mom, should you be doing that?" Annie asked, rushing over to the stove.

"Annie, I'm fine," Mom said, humming as she broke eggs into the big skillet. "Didn't I tell you the ailment would go away?"

"Yes," Annie said slowly, studying her mom.

"You put up the dinner pails while I feed the boys," Mom said. "Then you and Grace and I will have some breakfast together."

"But I'll be late for school if I wait to eat with you and Grace," Annie said as she slipped her pinafore on over her dress.

Mom shook her head. "Annie, we've got us a warm spell for this time of year, and there's fall cleaning to do. We may not get any more days like this."

"Yes, Mom," Annie said, going to the pantry. It didn't seem fair that she had to miss school for fall cleaning. Still, she thought as she sliced meat from last night's roast, Mom was in high spirits today, and Grace would take an afternoon nap. . . . This was her opportunity. Today she would talk to Mom about high school.

Quickly Annie packed the dinner pails and ran out to the kitchen to watch for Miss Osborne to drive by. Usually the teacher was at the school a half hour before anyone else, and that meant she would be going by soon.

"What are you standing at the window for?" Mom asked.

Annie turned slightly so she could see Mom sitting at the table with the boys and Grace. "I want to give the teacher my homework," she said.

"I don't see why all the fuss over a little homework," Mom said. "Let the boys take it."

"Yeah, we can take it," Leo said, his mouth full of bread.

"Why can't we take it?" Ben said.

"Annie, you're staying home with me?" Grace asked.

"Here she comes," Annie said. She slid the homework from her geography book and hurried out the door. She clutched the papers and ran down the driveway. As the auto came closer, she waved her arms.

Miss Osborne pulled over to the side of the road and stopped. "Why, Annie, is something wrong?"

Annie stepped close to the auto. "I wanted to give you my homework. Mom is keeping me home to help with fall cleaning."

"Annie, I'm so sorry. We'll miss you," Miss Osborne said, taking the homework and placing it on the seat beside her.

"Usually I would hate to stay home," Annie said. "But Mom wasn't sick this morning. She even cooked breakfast." Annie leaned toward the teacher. "I'm going to ask her about high school."

"Oh, Annie, that is good news," Miss Osborne said. "I'll keep my fingers crossed for luck." She grabbed one of Annie's hands and squeezed. "I have to get to school now," she said, "but we'll talk more on Monday."

Annie stepped back and waved, watching as Miss Osborne drove away. Though it was a frosty morning, and only the willow trees along the creek still had leaves, Mom was right: already the sun was taking the chill off the air. Happily, Annie started back, shuffling through the piles of fallen leaves along the edge of the driveway. It would be a nice day—a very nice day.

When she stepped inside the kitchen door, the boys were coming out of the pantry, their dinner pails in hand.

"Lucky you," Leo said to her. "Wish Mom would keep us home."

"Well, I'm not," Mom said. "So off to school with you."

"Only girls get to stay home. Right, Mom?" Grace said.

"Girls and babies," Ben said, sticking out his tongue at Grace.

"Ben!" Mom gave a light swat on the backside.

"Let's get out of here, Leo," Ben said, slamming the door as they went out.

"That boy," Mom said, shaking her head. "He is a handful. Now then, the womenfolk can have some breakfast in peace and quiet."

"Am I a woman, Mom?" Grace said. "Annie, are you a woman? What are we having for breakfast? Ben and Leo ate up all the eggs and home fries."

"Almost peace and quiet, you mean," Annie said, and she and Mom laughed together.

After breakfast was over and the dishes were washed up, Annie started working, stripping the beds in the upstairs and bringing the soiled sheets to her mother. Mom had heated water on the stove, and when Annie came downstairs she lifted the heavy pots and poured the hot water into the washtubs over the sheets and soap shavings. While the sheets soaked, Annie took the quilts and wool blankets and hung them on the clothesline to air. She and Mom were busy the whole morning just doing the wash.

When the sheets were scrubbed, Annie brought in the bedding and hung the sheets on the line to dry. Grace stayed with her every second like a flea on a dog's back. After a while Annie just shut out her sister's chatter and thought about going on to school. She tried to imagine what Latin might be like. Miss Osborne had said once in class that Latin was a dead language, but the Romans had spoken it many centuries ago, and much of English came from Latin roots. Annie sighed. There was so much she didn't know.

When Annie walked into the kitchen after hanging out the wash, Mom was putting loaves into the oven. "That should do it for a while," Mom said, straightening. "We'll have a bite to eat now."

Later, after Mom put Grace in the downstairs bedroom for a nap, Annie made some chamomile tea, and she and Mom took their cups out to the porch. Mom settled in the rocker, and Annie sat nearby on the top step of the porch in the afternoon sun.

"I do so enjoy having you around, Annie. Next year we'll have more time together. We can do so many things—quilting—quilting is no fun alone. And you should be learning to make bread and sew your own

clothes. I get so much pleasure out of your company."
Mom sat back in the rocker and sipped her tea, her
face peaceful and happy.

Annie watched her mother's face, knowing her
mother was planning for *their* good times together
next year. Annie bit her lip and looked away. How
could she say something about high school now? But
she had to. When would she ever get a better chance?
Besides, what would Miss Osborne think if she didn't?

"Umm . . . Mom?" Annie said. "Maybe I could go to
school next year."

"What?" Mom said, leaning forward. "School? Why,
Annie, you've gone as far as you can. What more could
you learn going back to eighth grade?"

"Not eighth grade, Mom. I meant high school."

Mom sat rocking and rocking. "Guess you'd better
see if the sheets are dry. We've got to make up the
beds," she said.

"Mom, what about high school?" Annie said. She
stood up and leaned against a porch post.

"It's a silly notion, that's what I think. You'd have to
leave home. You've got plenty of schooling, plenty
enough for any girl. One thing I don't need is another
foolish Mae flitting off thinking some big future is out
there waiting for her." Mom stood up.

"I wouldn't be running away. Couldn't you at least
think it over, please? I really want to go. I really want
to learn more. There's so much for me to learn," Annie
said.

"There's plenty of time to think on it—next fall is far off. But just now we have plenty of work to put our backs to."

"Yes, Mom. I'll go get the sheets now," Annie said as her mother disappeared into the house.

Annie walked slowly to the clothesline, tears burning in her eyes. Maybe she had picked the wrong time to ask. But when was a right time? It seemed the luncheon with Miss Osborne couldn't have happened, or had happened only in a wonderful dream or in the words of a song that sang her to sleep at night. What would she say to Miss Osborne on Monday? How could she face her?

* * *

On Monday when Annie walked into the schoolroom, Miss Osborne rushed toward her and drew her over to the recitation bench in the corner. "Annie, what is it? What happened? Didn't you ask?"

"Miss Osborne, I did. . . . I did ask," Annie said. "Mom said it was a silly notion, and she's made all these plans for things she and I will do next year when I'm home all the time. . . ." Annie stopped to choke back the tears.

Miss Osborne put a hand on her arm. "I see," she said slowly. "Not only is your mom depending on you to help, she is looking forward to your companionship as well. Hmmm . . . this must have been a shock to her."

"What should I do?" Annie asked.

Miss Osborne thought for a minute. "My guess is that your mom needs some time to get used to the possibility that you might not stay at home. Give her some time—several weeks at least—then ask her again. Perhaps she'll be more receptive then," she said.

Annie didn't think that all the time in the world could make a difference to Mom. What she needed was a miracle like Moses parting the Red Sea for the Hebrew children to escape Egypt.

"I've got just the antidote for you," Miss Osborne said with a laugh. "I've brought you a book by Dickens. I'm sure you'll find his writing most entertaining." The teacher moved the few short steps to her desk and picked up a book thicker than a Bible. "I have a feeling that you will enjoy this very much," she said, handing Annie a copy of *David Copperfield*.

Annie took the book and set it carefully on top of her schoolbooks. Her heart beat faster. "Thank you," she said, eager to get to her seat and begin reading.

"There are so many other books I'd like to share with you," Miss Osborne said. "But go on, go ahead and start reading. There's still some time before general assembly."

NINE

"ingle bells! Jingle bells! Jingle all the way!" Grace fairly screeched. An afternoon snow squall had set everyone in the Christmas spirit; the world outside was swirling with the cold white flakes. Ben and Leo had long since bundled up and run out to play.

Annie sat quietly reading *Great Expectations* in Dad's chair in the corner of the kitchen near the window. It was one of the books Miss Osborne had lent her. She would have gone to her bedroom, but the upstairs was much too cold; some days the frost never thawed off the windows. It was a treat to sit and read for once. Mostly her studying had to be done during recess time at school. Annie smiled. They were the best times. Miss Osborne would often come and sit next to her to talk about books. The teacher would put questions to her, questions that had to be thought out, like "Was Uriah Heep the darker self of David Copperfield?" How would she ever have considered such things if the questions had not been asked? It was all so new and wonderful.

How quickly those pleasant hours of school had

flown by; already Christmas was just ten days off. The house had taken on the spicy smell of lebkuchen just after Thanksgiving, and Mom had finally gotten over being sick every morning and had been sparkling with secrets for the past few days. Annie had heard the sound of the sewing machine treadle going till late the past several nights, after she was in bed. Even now Mom was busy with her knitting needles making something for Dad while he was out at the barn.

"Jingle bells! Jingle bells!" Grace stood in front of her now. "Come on, Annie. Sing with me, please?" Grace's face was flushed with excitement. "Sing with me, Annie."

Annie sighed. Pip was just going to Miss Havisham's, and she was eager to learn what would come of it, but she laid down her book and let Grace pull her to her feet.

Christmas was, after all, for children, and Grace was the only one of them who still believed in Santa Claus. Annie knew what she'd be getting for Christmas. It was the same every year—a flannel nightie, cotton stockings, green wool socks and mittens, and long underwear. On Christmas Eve Dad would go fetch Grammie Martin from the coal flats by the river in the village. Grammie would bring them walnuts and oranges and peppermints for their stockings from Woodmansee's General Store in South Branch, where she worked.

Annie loved having Grammie Martin come, and she

loved getting the warm new clothes, but even now, with Christmas so near, her thoughts were about high school—about becoming a teacher. She tried to study every spare minute, but it seemed as if the supper dishes were no sooner washed up than it was time for bed, and her bedroom was too cold for doing anything but sleeping, even if she was allowed to take up a lamp.

Mom put down her knitting and came to stand next to Annie and Grace by the window. They stood silently, watching as the snow fell and drifted across the north field.

"Let's sing 'Deck the Halls,'" Mom said. She slipped an arm around Annie's waist and started to sing.

Annie joined in, but she sang softly. Her own voice wasn't pleasing like Mom's. It was too low for singing melodies, and she struggled along just a bit off key.

When they finished the chorus, Mom leaned her head on Annie's shoulder. "You're such a comfort to me, Annie, a real blessing. Goodness knows, how would I ever manage without you?"

Annie swallowed. The setting sun broke suddenly through the snow showers. "Look, Mom, the sun. It's going to stop snowing."

"I don't want it to stop snowing. I don't want the snow to go away," Grace said. She scowled and stuck out her lower lip.

Mom dropped her arm from Annie's waist and went back to her chair by the stove. Mom hadn't been sick mornings lately, but Annie had noticed how she'd stopped wearing the belt on her housedresses and how, when she sat down, she eased herself slowly into a chair. Just last week Dad had brought one of the big cushioned chairs from the parlor and put it by the stove for Mom.

"Guess you might as well keep on reading that book Miss Osborne lent you. Wouldn't mind if you read a bit of it out loud till we start supper."

"Read to us, Annie," Grace said, climbing into the big chair with Mom.

"I took a peek in that book of yours. Dickens wrote that book, didn't he," Mom said. Her fingers moved surely and quickly, the needles clicking even as she talked. "He's the one that wrote that story *A Christmas Carol*. My pa always read that to us come Christmastime. It's a shame none of my children ever got to know him. He was a wonderful man, my pa. And such a voice. You never heard the likes. How he could mimic that old Scrooge." Mom laughed, and her face seemed younger somehow. "Would Miss Osborne have that *Christmas Carol,* Annie?"

"I don't know, Mom. I'd be glad to ask." Annie paused and watched Mom's face brighten as she was taken up with her memories. "Tell me more about Grandpa Martin," she said.

Mom stopped and looked down to count her stitches and then took up her knitting again. "My pa was your only grandparent that had much schooling. He went clear to the eighth grade same as you," Mom said proudly. "Me and your dad only got to fifth grade. We were needed to help out at home. Guess we weren't needing to learn more anyway."

Annie nodded. She'd heard the part about Mom and Dad enough times, but she'd never known about her grandpa. Annie gazed out the window. The snow hadn't quit. Ben and Leo were rolling snowballs and making forts in the field. "More than likely my grandpa would've gone to high school, if he'd had a choice."

"Why I should say he would've, had there been any high schools close by," Mom said.

Annie looked down at the book lying open on her lap. The daylight was fading. It was hard to see the print. "Mom . . . I . . . I . . ." Annie's voice faltered.

"Why, Annie, what is it?" Mom asked.

Annie took a deep breath. "Mom, remember when I asked about going to high school? Do you think I might?" she said, all in a rush.

Mom dropped her knitting in her lap. A troubled look passed over her face, and she slid her eyes away from Annie to Grace. Grace had fallen asleep. Mom brushed the sweaty ringlets back from the little girl's forehead. "Town is no place for children. Remember how Mae talked about the bootlegging and the bank robbers with guns? You'd be so far away, and I depend on you so," Mom said, her eyes filling with tears. "How could I ever get on without you?" Mom sat quietly for a second and seemed to be considering.

"Well, if it's the Lord's will, Annie," she said with a deep sigh. "Let me pray on it a bit. Let's wait and see what the Lord reveals."

Annie slumped against the chair back, and stared down at the book in her lap. *If it were the Lord's will,* she knew well enough by now, really meant *if it were Mom's will,* and like as not God wouldn't have any say at all. Schooling was fine, but helping out at home was more important, and *she* was a girl. Girls didn't need much book learning. Hadn't she heard Mom and Dad say that often enough?

"It's getting dark. I'd best trim the lamps," Annie said. She closed the book on Pip's adventure and moved to the table. How would Mom decide what the Lord's will would be? Annie glanced over at her mother. The knitting still lay in her lap. Mom was smiling and watching Grace as she slept. Annie had the unwelcome feeling that the new baby coming might have something to do with the Lord's decision.

TEN

T he sky was overcast and gray, and the branches of the trees were white—a sure sign of snow, Dad would say.

Annie squinted in the poor light of the schoolhouse. It was hard to see from where she sat, in the middle row of seats farthest from the windows. She stared at the arithmetic problems in her book, but this morning the figures wouldn't stick in her mind at all.

Miss Osborne had sent Ben and two of the older boys out to the hemlock woods behind the school to pick out a tree. Ben could be heard shouting out orders. Everyone fidgeted and glanced continually toward the windows on the north side, waiting for a glimpse of the tree.

Ben's voice was suddenly louder and nearby. "'Fifteen men on a dead man's chest—Yo-ho-ho, and a bottle of rum!'"

Miss Osborne paused midlecture and looked toward the window. The second grade reading group on the recitation bench tittered.

Annie closed her arithmetic book. It was no use.

She couldn't keep her thoughts on schoolwork. Christmas was only four days off, and there was too much going on.

She pulled *A Christmas Carol* from her desk. When she had come into the schoolroom that morning, Miss Osborne had handed her the book. It wasn't schoolwork, but she was eager to get a look at it, this story her Grandpa Martin had loved and read to Mom and her sisters. Annie opened the book and found herself pulled in by the picture of a snowy London on the first page. She ran her fingers over the fancy lettering that read *STAVE ONE   MARLEY'S GHOST.* Woven about it were holly and ivy. It was beautiful. Imagine owning such a book. Imagine giving such a gift to Mom.

The boys banged in through the door and pulled the tree behind them. It was ready to be stood up, the boys having already nailed a crosspiece of wood to the stub of its trunk.

"It's a lovely tree," Miss Osborne said, clasping her hands and watching as they stood it up near her desk. Miss Osborne drew in her breath. "Oh, but the hemlock has such a pleasing fragrance," she said, gazing at it. "I think . . . I think we shall take the rest of the morning to finish the cards to our parents. If you have that completed, you may hang your trimmings on the tree."

The school was at once alive with bustle and chatter. Annie looked back at her open book. She really should finish her card for Mom and Dad, but already she was drawn into the story.

"Annie?" Miss Osborne slipped into the empty seat beside her. "There's been so much Christmas excitement this past week, I'm sorry I haven't had any time to spend with you."

"I asked Mom about going to high school. . . . I did, just last Saturday. She said . . . she said . . . she didn't say no."

Miss Osborne pressed her hand. "Annie, I'm so glad you asked before Christmas break, but what did she say?"

Annie lowered her head. "Mom said she'd pray about it. See if it's the Lord's will. That's how Mom is about everything."

"But that's good news!" Miss Osborne said.

"Really?"

The teacher nodded. "How could it be anything but the Lord's will?"

Annie bit her lip. It could easily be Mom's will, but she couldn't say that to the teacher. "I guess you're right."

"Yes, I am. Now stop worrying so much," she said, standing up. "I'd better create a little order; the Christmas spirit is getting a bit out of hand, but we'll talk soon. I'm eager to learn what you think of *Great Expectations.*"

Annie wished she could feel as positive as the teacher, but Miss Osborne did not know Mom.

"Annie?" Aletha plunked down into the empty seat

beside her. "Where'd you get that book?"

"I borrowed it from the teacher," Annie said.

"Oh." Aletha leaned closer. "I need help with my card, Annie. Could you help me?"

Annie sighed and closed the book. "Of course. What's the trouble?" Carefully she slid the book back into her desk.

Aletha held the red folded construction paper against her chest.

"Well, it might help if you showed it to me."

Aletha brought the card away from her bosom.

"Why, it's a lovely Christmas scene, Aletha," Annie said.

Aletha grinned and bobbed her head, but the worried look was soon back on her face. "Can't think of nothing to write my ma and pa."

"Oh," Annie said. She should have known that would be the hardest part for Aletha.

Ben and several of the other children were trying to hang strings of popcorn and cranberries on the tree, but Justine was bossing everyone, insisting the strings be draped on in a certain way. Justine had even brought in a box of ornaments, colored glass balls, "bought from Woolworth's Department Store in Bradford," she had bragged to Annie and Aletha on the way to school that morning.

Ben was beginning to look vexed. Annie could tell by the set of his jaw that he was sick of Justine's giving orders like a queen.

"Annie?"

"Hmmm?" Annie looked away from the Christmas tree and back to Aletha's card. She opened it. Inside Aletha had written *Merry Christmas to Ma and Pa.* "That's a good start," Annie said. "Maybe, well, think about what the best thing is your ma and pa do for you."

Aletha squinched up her eyes. "Uh . . . um . . . they're always nice to me, and they don't holler when I don't know how to do things." Aletha sniffed and stared at Miss Osborne. There were times when the teacher wasn't too patient with Aletha.

"Very good," Annie said. "Now just write on your card what you told me."

Aletha looked at Annie with wonder. "Why, I did that real easy, didn't I?"

"Miss Osborne!" Justine shrieked, stamping her foot. "Make Ben stop singing that filthy song. Make him stop!"

Ben was singing "Yo-ho-ho, and a bottle of rum!"

Ben grabbed one of Justine's silver balls from the tree. "Justine, you h-h-hussy, you rotten hussy!" he shouted and dashed the ornament to the floor.

Justine broke into sobs. Everyone else was perfectly quiet and still. Miss Osborne's face was turning deep red.

Annie shuddered. How could Ben say such an awful thing?

"Ben Lucas, you will apologize to Justine and the

whole school this very instant, or . . . or I will have to punish you."

"I won't. Go ahead and thrash me. I ain't sorry."

Miss Osborne picked the heavy ruler off her desk. "Come stand over here, Ben Lucas." Her voice shook with anger, but a look of fear passed over her face.

Ben strode over to her. "Well, give it to me," he said.

Miss Osborne whacked him a half dozen times on his backside, but Ben never flinched. He just looked up at her and smirked.

The rest of the school day was dismal. Annie couldn't wait for the day to be over, for everyone to leave, so she could apologize to Miss Osborne for Ben's actions. Miss Osborne had never hit anyone before.

When school was over that day, Annie stayed in her seat until everyone had left. She approached the teacher's desk slowly. Miss Osborne would be leaving in a couple of days to spend the Christmas holidays with her folks. What if she told them about Ben? The Osbornes would think the Lucases were a horrid family. They might even change their minds and not want a Lucas to board with them.

"I'm sorry my brother acted up that way. "He's . . . he's . . ."

"Very defiant," Miss Osborne said, her voice cold and sharp. She dipped her pen in the inkwell and began writing on someone's school paper. "I've never hit anyone before in my life. I least expected it to be one of your brothers."

Annie hadn't known what to expect, but not this. "I am truly sorry," she said.

Miss Osborne nodded. "You will tell your father. He should know," she said, staring up at Annie.

Annie swallowed. How could she tell Dad? "I guess . . . yes, I will," Annie said, feeling bitterly torn. She left the schoolhouse feeling sick at heart. One small matter had changed her life so quickly. The schoolyard was empty. She started slowly down the road toward home.

When she was out of sight of the school, Ben sprang suddenly from the brush alongside the road. "Annie?"

She sniffed and didn't answer him.

"Annie, you gonna tell Mom and Dad?" Ben's face was white with worry.

"Look here," Annie said, turning on him. "I don't hold to name-calling or being disrespectful to the teacher. I have half a mind to thrash you myself. You've gone and spoiled everything for me!" Annie stopped and grabbed the rough brown wool of Ben's coat. She yanked him up close to her face. "What do you think I'm going to do?" She dropped the material and pushed him away from her. Tears streamed down her face. Lord, why did life have to be so hard? Ben stared at her, his eyes wide and frightened.

"I won't tell," she said, wiping her cheeks with the sleeve of her coat. It would spoil Christmas for the whole family if she told. She couldn't do it; it wasn't right to tattle on your kin. "But you best never act that way in school again, Benjamin Lucas. You hear?"

"I . . . I didn't mean to do wrong, Annie. Honest."

She was surprised to see that Ben's eyes were filling with tears. Annie swallowed. "You were right not to apologize. Saying you're sorry means nothing—nothing when it's not true," she said.

They walked the rest of the way home in silence.

Eleven

It was Christmas Eve. Annie held Grace close to her—it took so long for the bed to get warm, even with the heavy quilts and the irons heated on the stove and wrapped in flannel for their feet.

Downstairs there was still the rustle of movement and crackle of paper. Dad and Mom and Grammie Martin were talking in hushed tones as they went about filling the stockings and putting the decorations on the tree.

"Annie?" Grace was especially squirmy and wide awake. "When will Santa Claus come? Will he bring me a doll? Annie?" Grace reached over and patted her face.

"Yes, if you've been a good girl—real good," she added, just in case Grace didn't get one.

Grace was quiet for a minute. "Annie? Can you tell me that story about the night before Christmas, but let me say the reindeer, Annie, please?"

"If you settle down. Promise to settle down. Santa won't come until you go to sleep."

Grace gave a huge sigh. "I promise."

"'Twas the night before Christmas, when all through the house, not a creature was stirring, not even a mouse. . . .'" Annie could feel Grace's body going limp beside her. By the second time through the poem, Grace was at last breathing deeply. Grace never got tired of any of the Christmas stories. She had hobbled about all week like Tiny Tim, crying "God bless us every one!" Even Ben had seemed a bit softened up by Tiny Tim when Annie had read the story aloud to the family.

Annie had prayed that Miss Osborne wasn't still mad at the Lucases because of Ben, and the teacher had squeezed her hand and wished her a Merry Christmas at school dismissal the last day. "After the holidays, when things have settled down, we'll get back to our plans again," she had said. So maybe the teacher had forgiven them, but Annie wondered. Christmas had a way of making people feel more kind than usual.

If only Mae could come for Christmas. Maybe Elmer would bring her out tomorrow. Perhaps Mae could help her find a place to board in town. . . .

Annie was startled to hear the chugging of an automobile and the crunching of tires as it came up the drive on the crusty snow. Annie sat up. Who could be coming this time of night? It must be nigh on ten o'clock. She slipped from the bed and hurried to the window. She knelt down on the floor and drew up the shade. The pane was thickly coated with ice and frost. She scratched at the frost with her fingernail but it didn't help; Annie stuck out her tongue and pressed it against the glass until she had an oblong hole to peer through.

It was Mae! Mom had said that because of the snow-storm yesterday, Mae wouldn't make it for Christmas. Mae was alone. She must have driven out in one of Elmer's autos.

Annie heard the kitchen door slam and Russell and Dad stamping their feet on the porch. Mae was climb-ing out of her auto. Dad held up the lantern and walked out to meet her. Annie could hear Mae's voice tinkling like a little bell in the cold night as she grabbed Dad and hugged him.

The auto was full of parcels and something in a huge crate just barely fitting into the back. Annie watched as Dad and Russell struggled to get it out. What had Mae gone and bought them?

Annie shivered, not from feeling the cold, but from the forgotten pleasure of Christmas secrets that just now touched her. She looked up at the moon, its white light glowing on the crisp snow. She half-ex-pected to see a sleigh and eight tiny reindeer.

They were inside now and talking again in low voices. Annie climbed back into bed and snuggled up to Grace for warmth. The heat was gone from her iron; she drew her feet up into her nightgown. It was hard to stay in bed knowing Mae was downstairs and hearing her voice so filled with life and sudden laughter.

"Annie?" Ben called softly. He and Leo appeared in her doorway.

"Is Mae here?" Leo asked.

"Yes, but what are you doing out of bed?"

"We can't sleep," Leo said.

"And there's all that racket going on," Ben said.

Annie sat up, being careful not to disturb Grace. "I can't sleep either. Why don't you boys get a quilt and come in on my bed. But be quiet about it."

They were back soon and wrapped up in their quilts on the foot of her bed.

"What did Mae bring? Did you . . . ow! Move your iron, would you, Annie?" Leo said, rubbing his backside.

"Did you see what she brought?" Ben finished.

Annie was about to tell them that Mae had brought something in a big crate when the sound of music came wafting up the stairs.

"What the . . . ," Ben said.

"Shhh," Annie said. They were quiet, listening. "Si-i-lent night, ho-o-ly night . . ."

"Mae's gone and got us one of those music machines," Ben squealed.

"A Victrola," Annie said.

"Yeah, that's it. Let's go down, Annie. Please, can we?" Leo asked.

"Well, not without Grace. She's asleep."

"Bah! Humbug!" Ben said. He poked Grace with his foot. "Hey, Grace, Santa Claus is here. Want to see him?"

"Be-en," Annie said, but not too sharply.

"Come on, Grace," Leo said. "Santa Claus."

Grace sat straight up. "Santa Claus?" Even in the dark Annie could tell that Grace's eyes were wide with wonder. "Oh! He's playing music," she said.

Ben and Leo broke into giggles. "Come on, Annie. Mom and Dad won't holler," they pleaded.

Annie pulled Grace into her arms and the lot of them rushed down the stairs to the parlor.

"What took you so long?" Mae asked, shaking her glorious golden hair. She and Russell were standing in the corner by the stairwell next to the new Victrola.

Leo and Ben rushed over. Ben circled around the dark redwood cabinet, watching the record spinning around. "How does it work, Mae? Show me how it works," Ben said.

"Where's Santa Claus?" Grace asked as Annie put her down. "Oh!" She stared at the tree, decorated now with the presents wrapped up in green and red tissue paper. Some were hanging; some were placed on the branches. The biggest presents were underneath the tree. Annie didn't think she had ever seen so many presents for the Lucases before.

Dad had built up the fire in the parlor stove, and the room glowed with light from the lamps. Mom and Grammie Martin sat on the davenport and smiled.

"Looks like Santa came, Grace. You must have been a good girl," Grammie said.

"You kids might as well have your Christmas, long as you're up," Dad said.

The boys and Grace squealed with happiness. Annie whooped a bit herself, but she thought no one heard, not with all the scrambling to the tree.

There was a present all wrapped up pretty with ribbon under the tree. The tag read "For Annie From Mae and Elmer." Annie's fingers shook as she forced herself not to tear the paper. It was a dress, a beautiful cranberry red with a dropped waistline like Miss Osborne wore.

"Bought in Fowler's Department Store," Mae said. "Go try it on, Annie. You can take one of the lamps."

"They must pay you real good at that job of yours," Grammie said, looking proud with the soft blue shawl Mae had given her thrown over her shoulders.

"Oh, Grammie, it was nothing. I bought the Victrola on time. Just a small down payment and then almost nothing a month. Elmer insisted I do special for my family."

Russell was cranking up the Victrola again. He grabbed Mae around the waist, and they sashayed about the room. Leo and Ben were busy playing with their new farm sets, arranging them under the tree.

Mom's face was peaceful. Annie watched as she looked at each one of her children. When her gaze rested on Annie, Annie smiled. She longed suddenly to be swept into Mom's arms the way Grace was—Grace so contented, cuddling her new baby doll.

Annie gathered up her dress, took a lamp from its stand, and went to Mom and Dad's bedroom off the parlor. She pulled off her nightgown and stepped into her new dress. The wool was so soft; it was a pleasure to feel it. Even against her bare skin it wasn't scratchy.

Annie stood in the dim light thinking suddenly of *A Christmas Carol,* of the boy and girl peering out from the robe of the Ghost of Christmas Present as his time with Scrooge was drawing to an end. She had read the passage over and over: "This boy is IGNORANCE. This girl is WANT. Beware them both, and all of their degree, but most of all beware this boy, for on his brow I see that written which is DOOM, unless the writing be erased." Annie pressed her palms against her blazing cheeks. If she stayed here, her life would become as awful as Mom's. She had to leave; she had to go to high school. Somehow, she would do it.

Annie went back out to the warmth of the parlor and set the lamp back on its stand. When she turned around, Mae exclaimed, "Why, Annie!" She clapped her hands together. "That cranberry, it's truly your color!" Mae stepped up close and fussed with Annie's hair. "My, my, you're going to be a looker yet," she said.

Twelve

It was after midnight before the Christmas festivities quieted down and they were all back to bed. Grace was soon asleep, and Annie slipped into bed next to her. Mae stood in front of the bureau mirror and pulled pins from her hair.

"Mae?" Annie said. "The dress you gave me, is it like the dresses the town girls wear—a . . . a schoolgirl my own age? I was wondering what they look like."

Mae slipped her nightgown over her head and began brushing her hair. "I don't know, Annie. I don't pay attention to girls much," she said. Mae laid the brush on the bureau and slipped into bed on the other side of Grace. "When I saw that cranberry wool, I said to myself, 'That is my Annie's color, sure as I live and breathe.' I truly have an eye for clothes," Mae said.

"Mae?" Annie paused. "You have a lot of girlfriends at the factory, and you know people from church. Maybe, well, could you ask around, see if any families board girls? Mae, if I stay here, I'm going to end up like Mom. I want to go to high school. I want to be—"

Mae burst into giggles and bounced the bed a bit,

making the springs creak. "Annie, I've just got to tell you. I've been itching with it all night."

"Mae!" Annie said. "But what about—"

"Oh, Annie, I'm sorry, but just let me tell you this one thing. I have to tell you and then you can have a turn, but this is just too important." Mae stopped and took a deep breath. "Annie, me and Elmer set the date for January the twenty-second. We are getting married!" Mae said, squealing into the bedcovers.

Annie closed her eyes. Elmer again. She might have known.

"Annie, Elmer's got this cute little house all picked out and a down payment on it. You'll have to come and see us sometime. You can wear the dress I bought you. Me and Elmer will drive you all around and take you to Fowler's and Woolworth's. . . . Oh, Annie, tomorrow Elmer's coming out for Christmas dinner. You are going to meet him at last." Mae lowered her voice. "He's going to ask Mama and Daddy for my hand. This is the most real excitement of my entire life. It is too wonderful."

"Wonderful, clearly wonderful," Annie said, feeling disgusted.

Mae shook her head. "Annie, you are so funny. Someday you're going to feel this way. See if you don't, and Elmer was just saying to me . . ." Mae paused. "Are you listening to this, Annie? This is real important. Annie?"

"Yes, Mae."

Mae sighed. "Elmer says I am not to work one bit more in that factory. I am to quit just as soon as our vows are said. Elmer's so sweet on me, Annie."

"Mae? Mae, I need you to help me."

Mae yawned. "I am plumb tuckered out. I best get my beauty rest. Can't let Elmer see me with rings under my eyes. But we can talk tomorrow. Why, we'll have lots of time before Elmer comes," Mae said, turning over on her side, away from Annie.

Lots of time? Had Mae already forgotten what a lot of work it was just to feed them all? And she still had her regular chores—emptying the slops and filling the lamps and making up the beds and . . . Would life never change?

Annie lay on her back and stared into the darkness. Mae was all wrapped up in Elmer and getting married and living in a cute little house, but Mae had said she could come for a visit. Well, why not stay with them and go to high school? She wouldn't be a charity case that way . . . except Mom was in the family way, and who would do the extra chores? Annie sighed and curled her fingers into fists. It wouldn't be easy for Mom to let her go.

* * *

"Elmer! That's Elmer coming. I can tell," Mae said, scrambling out to the parlor and bobbing from window to window, the curtains billowing about her. "Oh, it is Elmer. Annie, quick, is my lipstick smeared?" She held her puckered lips up to Annie.

"No, Mae. It looks fine."

Russell laughed. "What a silly goose you are, Mae," he said. He and Dad were sitting on the davenport. Dad had dozed off and was snoring loudly. Even Mae's jumping about didn't wake him.

Russell reached out and grabbed Mae's wrist. "Gonna pucker up like that for Elmer?"

"Now, Russell, it's clear to me that you are jealous of Elmer, 'cause you don't have yourself a girl!" Mae said, yanking her wrist free. "Look at this place!" Mae dashed about in a flurry, straightening the Christmas clutter. "Can't let Elmer see the parlor looking like this. Oh, my pinafore, hang it up for me like a dear, would you, Annie?" she said. "I wouldn't want Elmer to think we were too old-fashioned. Take yours off, too, Annie," Mae said. She headed back to the kitchen, Annie close behind her.

"Goodness, Mama, can't you make those kids get away from the window? Mama! Oh, he's at the door already!" Mae wailed. She pushed past Mom and Grammie fixing dinner at the stove and ran to get the door.

"Now don't everybody gawk at him," she flung over her shoulder, before pulling open the door. "Why, Elmer, Merry Christmas. It is a pleasure to see you," she said, drawing him into the house. "Let me help you with your coat."

Ben and Leo and Grace had turned from the window and were staring at Elmer.

Elmer smiled. "You must be Ben and Leo and Grace," he said.

"You know me?" Grace said, pointing at him.

"I might," he said, a laugh in his voice. "Do you know me?" he asked, pointing at Grace.

Annie sighed. Elmer had such a pleasing voice.

Grace took a step closer to him.

"We know all about you," Ben said. "That's all *she* talks about." He crooked his thumb at Mae.

"Be-en . . . ," Mae said, her cheeks all rosy. She tugged at Elmer's arm. "You have to meet my mama and Grammie Martin." She scowled at the kids over her shoulder.

"Pleased to meet you at last, Elmer," Mom said, blushing. She straightened her shoulders and smoothed her hands over her stomach. She was wearing the new flowered housedress Grammie had made for her and the ruffled apron from Mae—"Not for everyday, just special for company," Mae had said. Mom bobbed her head, then turned back to the stove.

Grammie eyed him up and down. "A dandy-looking young man you are," she said, nodding her approval.

"That must be Annie," he said, noticing her finally. "The scholarly one," he added softly.

Annie's heart bumped queerly. Why, Elmer was handsome. His eyes were such a deep brown.

"She does love to read," Mae said, her voice all bubbly again. "You must meet Daddy and Russell." She linked arms with him and drew him toward the parlor.

The scholarly one, Elmer had called her. What a gentleman. Annie followed Mae and Elmer out of the kitchen and through the connecting hallway that led to the parlor. The younger ones had already danced ahead hollering out to Dad that Elmer was here.

"Annie. An-nie!" Mom called. "Grammie and I could use a hand. It's time to get the food on the table."

Annie turned back. She could hear Dad's voice and then everyone laughing, and she longed to run through the hallway door and join them in the parlor.

In no time at all the table was overflowing with the holiday foods, and everyone was crowded into the kitchen and seated around the table. Dad returned thanks a bit longer than usual, but soon they were filling their plates.

"Well, Elmer, we're glad to have you join our family for Christmas dinner," Dad said.

"Thank you, sir," Elmer said. He rubbed his hands together. "This is some feast, Mrs. Lucas," he said. He took the platter of ham from Russell and forked a big piece onto his plate.

Mom smiled and looked pleased. "Why, it's kind of you to say so," she said.

"I been wondering how good a living a man can make out there in town," Dad said.

"Well, sir," Elmer said. He gave Dad a steady look. "I suppose you know I own a filling station and automobile repair shop."

"Ey-ah," Dad said, his fork poised over his plate.

"Looks to me as if the automobile business has a real bright future, Mr. Lucas. I do right well for myself."

Dad nodded. "Russell here likes to tinker," he said. "We got us a Chevy this year. Russell's been studying on it something fierce. Got to drag him away for chores."

"That right, Russell?" Elmer asked.

Russell nodded.

"Why don't we go out after dinner and give her a looking over," Elmer said.

"Yes, sir, Elmer," Russell said, pushing a mouthful of succotash into his mouth.

Annie didn't think she'd ever seen Russell so eager about anything before.

"I'd be pleased if you joined us, too, Mr. Lucas," Elmer said.

"Why, thankee, son," Dad said. "I have a mind to do just that."

It was plain the whole family was drawn to Elmer. Mae had gotten a good catch, all right. Annie stared at him, his face so pleasant; already he seemed like one of the family. Why, she could talk to Elmer herself about staying with them, when the time was right. . . .

Thirteen

everal months later in early April, Miss Osborne stood in the doorway of the schoolhouse and smiled and waved as Annie set off toward home.

It was one of those days when the very earth beneath Annie's feet seemed to rejoice. It was warm, and Annie slung her sweater over her shoulder and swung her arms, loving the way the fresh air and sunshine felt against her bare skin.

That afternoon Miss Osborne had given the eighth graders a trial test taken from some old high school entrance exams. Annie knew she had done well. Except for one or two arithmetic questions, she was sure she had answered everything correctly.

Annie slowed her steps to watch as a flock of bluebirds swooped into the tops of the willow trees alongside the road. Miss Osborne had often spent time with her during the dark winter days when it was too cold for outdoor recess. They would sit together and talk over "Evangeline" or *The Scarlet Letter*. The teacher always made her feel important, but she didn't speak to Annie about boarding with her parents or high school, other than to ask if Mom had reached a decision. Maybe the teacher's parents didn't want a Lucas to board with them. The teacher must have told them about the name Ben had called Justine and how he had laughed and hadn't apologized. Miss Osborne's cold voice and biting words because of Ben were still painful to remember.

Annie sighed and pushed away the troubling thoughts. It was too pleasant an afternoon to fret about school. Besides, Mae and Elmer had been married in January by the justice of the peace in Bradford and were now all settled in their own home. Several times that winter Mae had written letters brimming with the details of her new life.

Surely Mae and Elmer would board their own kin. Annie had no reason to worry over a place to stay, and, anyway, she still didn't know if Mom would let her leave home. Whenever she asked, her mom would say, "All in the Lord's good time. You can't rush the Lord, Annie. He'll give me a sign as clear as he did Moses with the burning bush."

Ka-ooga! Oo-ga! A horn blasted, and Annie jumped quickly off to the side of the road, then whirled to see who was coming. *Ka-ooga! Oo-ga!* It was Russell. He was driving their Chevy and waving an arm out the window. Clouds of red shale dust were flying up behind the auto.

"Annie! Annie!" he hollered as the Chevy came

closer. "Come on. Hop up," he called, a reckless glee in his voice.

Annie leaped onto the running board beside Russell and hung on to the door. "Sakes alive, Russell, you scared me half to death," she said, cuffing at him.

Russell grinned and ducked away from her. She laughed, too, and clung tighter as Russell stepped on the throttle.

How free she felt flying along so fast, her hair blowing back from her face, the warm April breeze slipping right by her.

"Got myself a job today," Russell said, hollering over the noise of the engine. "A job in town."

"A job in town?" Annie yelled. She'd never once taken it into her head that Russell wouldn't always be there on the farm working alongside Dad. She'd never known he longed to be anywhere else. "Well, I'll be . . . ," Annie said and gave a sharp whistle.

"I'll be . . . ," Russell said, nodding his head. "Thought you'd never see me moving out; thought I had roots right down into this rocky old ground; thought you was the only one with a dream, didn't you?" He bounced on the seat cushion and laid on the horn as they came in sight of the house.

The kids came swarming from the yard and running down the driveway to meet them. Russell never let up one bit on the horn. The kids were jumping about and hollering. Russell had a grin plastered on his face.

"Yes, sirreee," Russell crowed as he swung the

Chevy into the driveway and stopped. "I got myself a job, Annie."

Annie jumped off the running board, and even before Russell was out of the car, Ben and Leo and Grace were pressing up to the door. Even Mom had come out on the porch to see what the ruckus was about.

"What'd you bring us?" Ben demanded.

"Shouldn't have brought you anything, talking so rude," Annie said.

"Got something for you all." Russell whistled and reached through the window and drew out small brown bags with licorice sticks showing out of the top. He handed the bags around to the kids.

"How many licorice did you get?" Ben demanded of Leo as they hurried off to the backyard with Grace trotting behind.

Russell laughed and watched them go. His face looked burnt just as if he'd been out working in the wind all day, instead of being in town.

"Got some for you too, Annie," he said, reaching into the Chevy and grabbing up two more bags. "I know you don't like licorice," he said. "I brought you lemon drops and root beer barrels instead." He handed her the bag and studied her face. "Don't go saying nothing yet about my job, Annie," he said slowly.

Annie nodded and pressed the bag into the folds of her sweater. Tomorrow she would share the candies with Miss Osborne and Aletha and Justine.

Russell grabbed her wrist as she turned toward the house. "What do you think of me just going off and getting myself a job?" His face was still lined with laughter, but something in his voice bothered her.

Annie shook off the feeling. "Why, Russell, I think it's grand," she said.

He nodded slowly, seeming to consider, and turned toward the house. "Got you some chocolate drops," he called out to Mom as he walked toward her. "Shouldn't you be off your feet?" he scolded gently, giving her the bag.

Mom bent her head, looking pleased with the attention, and poked a chocolate into her mouth.

"Got lots of news from town and from Mae and Elmer. Wait till you hear."

"Mae? How's Mae doing? Nothing's wrong?" Mom asked.

"What's wrong? Who said anything was wrong?" he said, putting an arm across Mom's shoulder. "Mae's got a real nice home with Elmer and she's prettier than ever, but you'll have to hear the big news at supper," he said, swinging the screen door open. "High time I got to the barn." He grinned and disappeared into the house.

"Land sakes, that boy is a tease," Mom said, fretting with pride. She smacked her lips and fumbled in the bag for another chocolate. "I guess Mae's got herself a good life after all. I thought that girl would never get anything but heartache and trouble."

"You think I might take Grace and look for flowers in the woods?" Annie asked.

"There'd be time for that, I guess. I've been longing to see her," Mom said, leaning against Annie as they went into the house. "Time was, I could dash right over there myself, even in this condition."

"Mom, you ever dream about going places, being something when you was a girl?"

Mom folded down the top of the bag and tucked it into her apron pocket. "Why, I guess. I dreamed all the time about getting grown up and married and having babies . . . a whole passel of children, at least ten." Mom laughed as if this were the funniest thing ever. "I used to make up whole lists of names for my children. Never used a single one. I still have the list, though. It's in my Bible."

"What about now, Mom, do you ever dream now?"

Mom eased herself into the big cushioned chair by the cookstove and picked up a pan of potatoes she'd set aside. "Dreams are for young folks like you and Russell." Mom paused and started paring away. "Dream while you can, Annie. I reckon I'm too worn out from living my dreams to wish for anything different. What would I go wishing for, anyway, except maybe material for a housedress or a new handbag. What's done is done. No sense dreaming different now."

Annie turned toward the stairs. How could Mom bear her life—the work and babies and no dreams to live for?

"Mom?" Annie turned back. "I've been dreaming, you know, about going to high school. I've been studying all winter so I can make good marks on the entrance exams tomorrow, and I've been thinking how maybe Mae and Elmer would let me board with them or maybe Miss Osborne . . ." Annie stopped.

Mom looked up from her paring and smiled. "I know how you've studied and I haven't forgot. I've been praying and asking the Lord to show us a sign. The Lord will show us his will. Don't fear, child."

Annie came close to her mother's chair. It seemed hopeful that Mom had taken her dreams to heart all this while. "Mom?" Annie knelt down by the chair. "I've heard you and Grammie talk about putting out a fleece the way Gideon did in the Bible when he was seeking the Lord's will. You think you might do that for me?"

Mom pressed Annie's hand. "I was thinking that very same thing today. Why, all we need is a yes or no, I told the Lord."

FOURTEEN

Mom arranged the wildflowers that Annie and Grace had picked in a small glass and set it in the center of the supper table.

"Now, what's this news you were saving to tell us about Mae?" Mom asked Russell as they were passing the food at supper that night.

Russell took his time forking a couple of the steaming whole potatoes from the bowl in front of his plate and mashing them. "Well, now, all the while I been doing chores tonight, I've been figuring how Mae might be irked if I go telling her news. I suppose she might telephone and tell you her own self," he said, picking up the pepper and shaking a good bit of it on his potatoes.

Mom's face puckered up. "Russell, if there is something serious you are holding back about our Mae . . ."

"Now, Mom, you know how Mae gets all in a dither about things," Russell said.

"I know. I know," Mom said, looking vexed. "But there is no God-given reason to not be telling us."

"Guess I can tell you this much," Russell said,

rubbing his cheek and looking solemn. "I'm going to be an uncle." A grin spread clean across his face, and he tipped back in his chair. "Now what do you all think of that?"

Annie turned to Russell. "Why, it's truly thrilling." Annie smiled. Mae would likely come begging for her help.

"And you'll be a gramma, Mom," Russell said, his eyes still sparkling with fun. "Gram-maw Lu-cas."

It wasn't until that moment that Annie looked at Mom. Mom twiddled the flower she'd pulled through a buttonhole of her housedress and stared across the table, her face looking gray and heavy like an overcast sky.

"A gramma?" Grace said, pointing to Mom. "Will I be a gramma, too?"

"No, stupid," Ben snorted. "You can't be a gramma. You have to be really old, like Mom, to be a gramma."

"And fat," Leo said. "I bet even dumb old Aletha knows that."

"What do I get to be?" Grace whined.

Pain flickered in Mom's eyes, and Annie longed to protect her somehow. Getting old was never a part of the dream. Was that it? Annie felt shaken as she studied Mom's face. Mom was looking old. Some of her teeth were missing and her hair was streaked with gray. That would never happen to her. The Lord wouldn't will such a life on anyone.

"Yup. Mom's gonna be a gramma before long."

Russell laughed with pure enjoyment.

Dad reached over and rubbed Mom's arm. "Now, Esther, Mae starting a family of her own is purely a blessing from the hand of God."

Mom grabbed Dad's hand. Slowly, the grayness passed from her face.

"Mae's getting a family?" Grace began to laugh. "What does she need a family for? She's already got us."

"Russell has more news, don't you, Russell?" Annie said. She rose and reached past Russell for the blackberry pies on the sideboard. She smiled, thinking how soon her dream would come true. As soon as supper was over, she would talk to Mom about how much Mae would need her help, with the baby coming and all. Mom knew how flighty Mae was; she didn't know the first thing about caring for a baby. Annie set the pies on the table and began cutting them. She pictured herself sitting in a classroom at high school and bending over a book. She would work hard and be a real scholar; her whole family would be proud.

"I got myself a job in town today," Russell said.

"What's this about a job?" Dad asked, holding his plate out for pie. "How soon you going to start this job?" Dad didn't sound one bit troubled. Russell might have been discussing which heifers would be ready for calving this spring or the disrepair of the fences in the north pasture.

"Land sakes, Russell," Mom said. "How'd you

manage to get yourself a job in one day out to town?"

"Mom, I wasn't even asking around for jobs, just minding my own business, but I got myself offered one anyway." His voice took on a reckless glee.

"That's mighty odd," Dad said, wrinkling his forehead.

Mom clucked her tongue. "Now, Dad, anybody can tell what a good man our Russell is."

"True, true." Dad nodded his head.

"Don't anybody want to know what job I got?" Russell burst out.

"Tell us, son," Mom said.

"I am going to work in one of those filling stations, pumping gas and doing repairs on motors and engines and such."

Dad pushed back his plate. "Elmer says it's a real promising business."

"That's what he says." Russell grinned. "Told me that himself when he offered me the job. I accepted right off, since I know those two pesky fellas are old enough to take over my chores now," Russell said, jerking his thumb toward Ben and Leo.

"That's so," Dad said.

"Elmer? Mae's Elmer? He offered you a job?" Annie's hand shook, and she almost dropped the slice of pie she was putting on Ben's plate.

"Watch it," Ben growled.

"You know of any other Elmer?" Russell asked.

"Wh-where you going to be staying?" Annie asked.

104

"Would you let me tell the story, 'fore you go off asking questions?" Russell snapped. "Elmer told me himself how impressed he was with my knowledge of engines and all. Why, who would have thought my tinkering would have landed me a ca-reer?"

"Can't say I did." Dad held out his plate for more pie.

"Just thank the good Lord you'll be working with decent folk," Mom said. "When will he be wanting you to start?"

"After Easter. Just in time, too. You'll be needing the room for the new little one." Russell paused. "I guess you figured I'd be staying on with Elmer and Mae."

That's what Annie'd figured. She stared at the pie on her plate and clenched her hands into fists. She really hated Russell right then. He knew about her dreams. He had known all along, the way he sensed things about people, how she'd hoped to stay with Elmer and Mae.

The younger kids left the table and went off outdoors; the spring air was still warm, even as dusk settled in.

Annie got up and trimmed the lamps and began clearing the table. Russell kept on talking about *his* new career, and Mom and Dad sat silent, hanging on his every word.

"After a couple of years, I just might go into business for myself, and Elmer says he don't see why not. There's plenty of need for good mechanics, and he wouldn't consider it personal or anything. 'It's the American way,' Elmer says. He says he might even decide to make me a partner, expand the business some. Open another station, maybe. But I've been thinking, I might just get into this real estate business as well. It's raging something fierce. People are getting to be millionaires overnight. Lots of money to be made . . . real fast." Russell lapsed into silence, seeming to consider the prospect of being rich.

It must have been the most he'd ever said at one time. His voice rose and fell with the thrill of it; his face was lit with excitement.

It was clear that Mom and Dad were caught up in his dreams. They didn't seem one bit bothered that he was leaving home in a few days. Annie filled a pail with hot water from the tank on the stove, poured it over the soap shavings in the dishpan, and began to wash up the dishes. Why, Mom and Dad acted as if it were the most natural thing in the world to leave home. If Russell could do it, so could she. The only difference, as far as she could figure, was that she was too young, by Mom and Dad's way of thinking, and a girl, and there was no one to take over her chores.

Angrily Annie sloshed water from the dishpan as she scrubbed at the plates and looked at the stack of dishes still on the cupboard. If she had been a boy, no one would be worrying about what the Lord's will might be. Why, she would just go off and become a teacher, and Mom and Dad would sit right down and love it and act proud the way they were of Russell.

It all sounded so simple, listening to Russell talk about his plans, but for her nothing could be harder.

Annie watched out the pantry window as Ben and Leo raced past in the yard. Grace, clutching her doll, was calling out for them to wait up, but they were soon out of sight, swallowed up in the gathering darkness. Grace stared after where they had been and then turned, crying, and started toward the house.

No, it wasn't fair, and she had to do something about it for herself and for Grace.

Fifteen

I was awake the whole night just thinking about the exams today," Justine said to Annie and Aletha as they walked to school.

"I'm worried about arithmetic. I should've studied more. . . ." Annie broke off and chewed her lip.

Justine smoothed the skirt of her flowered chintz and sighed. "I don't see the reason for taking these exams. Why, I have the best grades in the school— and I do get so nervous taking tests. Sometimes I get so worried that I can't remember a thing. Father says not to let it bother me; I'll be going to high school no matter what."

Annie nodded. Of course Justine never had to worry. Somebody always looked out for her.

Justine smiled. "What about you girls? You planning on a higher education, hmmm?"

"Not me," Aletha said. "I ain't going to high school, and there's no good reason for the school board to make all the eighth graders take the entrance.

"Soon as I get through this year, I'm getting a housekeeping job with the Haineses. My ma says I can do the work of two horses."

Justine laughed. "What about you, Annie?"

"I'd like to," she said, wishing she had something to brag on, too. "Mom's thinking on it."

"Really?" Justine said, her eyes going wide. "Oh, speaking of your ma, my mother said to be sure and tell you that she'll be dropping off a box of clothes for your family someday this week from the Ladies Aid and also the sunshine basket for when the new baby comes. I told Mother to be sure and put a nice dress in for you. I figured you'd be needing something decent to wear for Easter Sunday."

"Thank you, Justine. That was truly thoughtful of you," Annie said sweetly, not wanting Justine to know how angry and shamed she felt. It was a relief to see the school as they rounded the last turn. Most of the kids were still running around outside, the morning being pleasantly warm and sunny.

The preacher's automobile was parked outside. He was substituting for Miss Osborne, since she would be taking them to the village for the exams.

Reverend Owens seemed to be a trifle impatient with Miss Osborne when Annie and Justine and Aletha walked into the schoolhouse. "Now, Olive, I think I am capable of running the school for one day. It isn't necessary to give me a lesson plan. After all, I've been preaching the word of God for seventeen years."

"Yes, Reverend Owens." Miss Osborne sighed. "You've dealt with boys, I'm certain. But they do have their tricks to play at times. . . ."

"Yes, yes," he said, waving his hand in a dismissing way. "You just run along now and let your mind be at rest."

"Fine then, yes." Miss Osborne picked up her handbag and a brown folder. There were bright red spots on her cheeks, and she held her head higher than usual. "Come, girls," she said, giving them a curt nod. "We mustn't be late."

As soon as they had all settled in the teacher's Ford, with Justine riding up front and the throng of waving kids left behind, Miss Osborne leaned back against the upholstery and sighed. "I do hope they will behave for Reverend Owens," she said, her lips twitching. "I did warn him, didn't I, girls?"

Annie smiled as Miss Osborne glanced back at her in the mirror. She figured the teacher wished the opposite, and she didn't blame her.

"Reverend Owens would personally speak to the parents of anyone who misbehaved. He wouldn't let any trouble-making boy off with just a paddling," Justine said, turning slightly, her gaze sweeping from Miss Osborne to Annie.

Annie saw Miss Osborne stiffen. "I brought us a treat for our special outing today," Annie said quickly, hitching forward and pulling the bag of candies from the pocket of her dress. What was Justine up to? Was she trying to suggest that Miss Osborne hadn't punished Ben enough, that the teacher should've gone directly to Mom and Dad? It would be just like Justine to recall for them all in great detail how Ben had smashed her precious Christmas ball and called her a nasty name. The last thing Annie wanted was any reminder to the teacher of that awful day. But why was Justine bringing it up now?

"You choose first, Miss Osborne," Annie said, holding the bag out to her teacher. "There's lemon drops and root beer barrels."

"You got that candy at Woodmansee's?" Justine asked.

"My brother Russell got them in Bradford yesterday. He's going to start working at a service station there right after Easter. He'll be staying with our sister Mae and her husband. Mae's . . . she's in the family way." Annie paused and held the bag out to Justine. Justine selected three of the lemon drops. "Her house is very small. Probably too small even for Russell to stay on after the baby comes," Annie said, sliding back and letting Aletha choose from the bag. She hoped Miss Osborne would remember that she needed a place to board. The teacher often mentioned high school, but why didn't she mention her parents' offer?

Annie stuck a root beer barrel in her mouth and leaned back against the seat. Everyone was quiet, except for Aletha crunching the candy in her teeth. Even Justine seemed to have run out of words for the moment, and Annie slid into a reverie of what the day might bring.

She began to feel nervous as they got closer to the village, but she was more excited than anything. She'd never been to the South Branch school before. It was the biggest in the district, with two big rooms, one for the lower grades and one for the upper grades. All the eighth graders in the school district would be taking the exam at South Branch, Miss Osborne had said.

"Please do your best today," Miss Osborne said as they drove into the village. "But don't get upset if there's anything you don't know. No one is expected to know everything. But at least *try* to answer all the questions," she said, glancing over the seat at Aletha.

Aletha moaned and chewed up the last of her candy.

Miss Osborne pulled her Ford in next to the other automobiles already parked near the school. She turned to the girls. "It is important to me, since I'm a new teacher this year, that my pupils have at least an average score. The school board might not want me back another year if you don't do well. But I have faith that you will," she said.

"Well, then, let us commence," Miss Osborne said with a sigh. She picked up her handbag and folder and pushed open her door. "Good luck on the exam, girls," she said, walking with them across the yard to the school.

Annie was surprised at how many eighth graders were in the school district; there must be thirty, maybe more. She took the desk assigned to her and looked

112

up and down the rows and counted the pupils. She was halfway around the room when she realized one of the boys was staring at her. His serious gray eyes were settled on her in a most uncommon way. He smiled and waved to her.

Annie smiled and waved back. It was the boy who had stopped his wagon for her the day she had gone to visit Miss Osborne. She stopped counting then and turned back around in her seat. A hot flush crept up her neck. Was her hair sticking out in an odd way? It always did have a mind of its own. Did he think she was funny looking? Clearly she did not have the pretty feminine look of Justine. Still and all, he had been a real gentleman that day, and maybe he just wanted to make friends.

Annie was glad when the exams were passed out and they were allowed to begin, after being lectured on the evils of cheating and the importance of budgeting their time. She broke the seal on her exam booklet and folded back the first page. . . .

Sixteen

A nnie worked steadily through the exam, only just aware of the rustle of movement as one of the teachers walked by her in the aisle from time to time. The test was much like the one Miss Osborne had given them the day before, but it was much longer, and Annie read over each question many times to make sure she understood it. Her hands shook as she wrote; it was important that she do better on this exam than she had ever done on anything, and she was worried even about the answers she knew were right.

Annie was surprised, when finally she had closed the exam booklet and laid down her pencil, that so much of the morning was gone; it was almost noon on the schoolhouse clock, and it seemed, as she glanced quickly about her, that most of the others were still working, except for the tall, gray-eyed boy. He had slouched down in his seat and appeared to be sleeping. She turned back and folded her hands on her desk.

Exactly at noon Mrs. Layton, the South Branch

teacher, ordered them to stop writing and put their pencils down. "Stay in your seats until all the exams have been collected," she said. "This afternoon we will do the arithmetic section. Make sure you are here promptly at one o'clock so that we may commence this final part of the exam."

When the exams had been collected, Annie, Justine, and Aletha rushed up to Miss Osborne at the front. "I was pleased to see how diligently all of you were working," Miss Osborne said, smiling.

"I read everything at least twice and thought and thought about the answers," Justine said. "I was very careful."

Annie nodded. "I thought on everything, too. It was hard not to worry, even about the easiest questions."

"Exams like these make all of us worry," Miss Osborne said. "But try to forget about the exam now, and go have your dinners. I'm staying here with the other teachers. We have plenty to talk over, too," she said with a small laugh. "Just get here quickly when the bell is rung."

Annie headed out of the schoolhouse with Aletha and Justine. As they made their way across the school-yard, Annie spotted the gray-eyed boy sitting with several other boys and a girl beneath a large, old elm.

"What did you think of all those questions on poetry?" Justine asked as they started toward Miss Osborne's Ford. "I declare, you would think Long-fellow was the only poet that ever lived."

"I'm glad I memorized all those passages from 'The Song of Hiawatha' and 'Evangeline.' It made it easier, but I still kept worrying that I was putting down the wrong answers," Annie said, pulling open the door of the auto.

Aletha shook her head. "More likely than not I got it all wrong."

They got their dinner pails from the Ford and found a large flat rock near the schoolyard and just a ways from the South Branch River, where they could eat their dinners. It was a mild day, and the rock had soaked up a good deal of warmth from the sun.

Annie sat down and dangled her feet off the side. She wasn't really hungry; she didn't even feel like talking. She glanced over toward the elm. The gray-eyed boy was talking, and everyone else was laughing.

"Annie . . . Annie?" Justine said.

Annie turned to the other girl. "Yes . . . what?"

"What did you think of the science part? I think the questions were too difficult, and really it wasn't a bit fair. We've never had much instruction in science," Justine said, dabbing with her hanky at the juice trickling on her fingers from the orange she was eating. "How did you do on that part, Annie?" Justine asked.

"The science, oh . . ." Annie shrugged. "It was the hardest part. But Miss Osborne did prepare us for it, Justine," she said.

Justine scowled. "Annie, you are so blind when it comes to the teacher. But then, you *are* the teacher's pet," she said, shooing flies away from her orange.

"I'm really not hungry for some reason," Annie said, putting her sandwich back in her pail. "I guess I'm just jittery about the arithmetic exam this afternoon. I think I'll take a walk by the river. Want to come?"

Aletha shook her head. "Can I finish your sandwich?" she asked.

"Please, go ahead," Annie said, holding out her pail to the other girl.

"I don't want to go either," Justine said. "I'm going back to the school. I can't stand these flies a minute more."

Annie headed for the river. She always liked the sound of water. How different the river was from the small creek that ran past their house. She might find some fossil rocks or colored stones for the boys and Grace. Annie picked her way over the rocks along the riverbank and searched for a colored stone or pebble.

"What are you looking for?" a voice behind her called.

Annie turned. It was that boy coming over the rocks toward her. He stopped when he was still a few yards away.

"Did you lose something?" he asked.

Annie shook her head and folded her arms across her waist. "I'm looking for fossil rocks," she said.

The boy grinned and stepped closer. "You're the

girl I saw last fall by the Perry place. You're a Lucas, aren't you?"

"Yes," Annie said, her face going redder than an overripe tomato. "Um . . . thank you for stopping your wagon last fall. I would've been covered with red dust if you hadn't. Thanks."

"You're welcome, Miss Lucas." He squatted down near her and tossed a piece of driftwood, mottled with dry grass, into the river. "So how did you do on the exam?" he asked.

"It was . . . well, it wasn't . . ." Annie stopped and took a deep breath. "I did quite well, thank you."

He laughed. "Most girls would never admit it."

Did that mean he thought her odd? "What about you?" she said. "I noticed you finished before anyone else. I figure the exam was easy for you."

"Or hard," he said. "Or maybe I didn't bother to answer *any* of the questions."

Annie jerked around to look at his face. Was he teasing? What sort of boy was he? "You mean . . . you didn't?"

He picked up a handful of small stones and started tossing them into the river. "I did quite well, thank you," he said.

Now he was mocking her. Annie bit her lip and watched as the stones hit the water.

"Look here," he said, turning a stone over in his fingers. "I've found me an arrowhead."

Before Annie could open her mouth, he stood up

and slipped the arrowhead into his pocket. She wished she had found it, but she was not about to ask him if she could see it. She started picking her way along the rocks of the shore.

"How do you like Longfellow's poetry, 'By the shores of Gitche Gumee' and all that?" he asked, trailing behind her.

"Longfellow is fine, but I like Whitman much better," she said.

"Come on, you never studied Whitman," he said.

Annie was on the bank now, and she swung around to face him. "I know what you're thinking. You're thinking a Lucas girl would never know about poetry."

"I didn't mean . . . look here, you don't have to get in a huff. I only meant that we aren't taught Whitman in school," he said, touching her arm.

One of the children was ringing the bell, and Annie turned and started toward the school.

He walked along with her. "Look, I'm sorry. What's your first name, anyway?"

"Annie," she said, going to the rock to get her dinner pail and sweater. "I . . . uh . . . I don't know your name either," she said, looking down, her face warm.

"I'm Lee . . . Lee Mosher. We have a farm on Spring Hill."

Mosher . . . Mosher . . . It must have been his mother who died in childbirth last fall. There were five children. The oldest was fifteen. That's what Uncle

Elton had told Mom. Annie thought of Mom then, how old and worn-out she looked, how hard it was for her to keep up with the chores. No, nothing was going to happen to Mom. "Are you planning to go on to high school?" she asked.

"Too much work at home," he said. "Otherwise, sure, I'd go."

"I might go," she said. "I want to be a teacher."

"A teacher?" He laughed. "Bet you won't. I'll bet you get married," he said.

"No, you're wrong. I never will!" she said as they walked into the schoolhouse. She hurried to take her seat, to get away from him, but he was right behind her and tugged a lock of her hair just as she got to her desk. "Will so," he whispered. Then, laughing, he walked back to his seat.

The afternoon passed slowly. Annie worked steadily through the arithmetic problems, but her thoughts kept flitting off to the Mosher boy behind her. He was the strangest boy she'd ever met. She couldn't decide if she liked him or not.

As soon as the exam was over and the booklets had been collected, Aletha and Justine rushed over to her.

"It's over. It's over at last! Just look at my hands," Justine said, turning up her palms to show the gray smears. "I never erased so much in my entire life."

"I got it all done, Annie, all the arithmetic," Aletha said. "Arithmetic is best—not so much reading."

"Arithmetic is not best," Justine said. "Is it, Annie?"

"Hmmm?" Annie slid from her chair and stood up. She looked quickly around her, but Lee was nowhere in sight. "What did you say, Justine?"

Justine's face colored. "Annie, I truly don't think—"

"Truly don't think what?" Miss Osborne asked as she joined them.

Justine shook her head and looked down.

Miss Osborne laughed. "Just don't tell me that you didn't pass," she said, moving toward the door.

"Oh, Miss Osborne," Justine said, hurrying after the teacher. "I'm positive *I* passed."

Annie looked about the schoolyard as they walked to the teacher's auto; she half-expected Lee to jump out from between the autos to mock her again. Thankfully, he didn't.

When they got to the teacher's Ford, Justine climbed quickly into the front and settled herself; Annie and Aletha got in the back. As they were starting to pull out of the schoolyard, Lee drove by with a big smile and waved.

Annie lifted her hand, smiled slightly, then rested her head against the back of the seat and closed her eyes. She didn't understand that Lee Mosher—one minute he taunted her, the next he was real pleasant. Why would a boy act that way?

Miss Osborne dropped Aletha off first and then Justine. After Justine had gotten out, the teacher looked back over the seat. "Why don't you ride the rest of the way up front, Annie? I know it's not far, but we can talk better that way."

Annie was pleased with the offer and quickly changed to the front. Miss Osborne backed out of the Pruetts' driveway and started driving slowly up the road.

"How was the exam?" Miss Osborne asked.

"Well . . . I don't want to sound boastful, but I did just fine, I think. And I checked everything. . . ." Annie glanced at her teacher, but she didn't seem to be listening.

"My parents are coming for a visit to the school on Good Friday. We have just a short session in the morning," Miss Osborne said. "I wanted to tell you privately, because they would like to stop by and meet your parents and formally invite you to stay with them."

"You mean . . . I mean . . . they're really going to ask me?" Annie squealed and bounced on the seat.

"Why, Annie, I'm pleased that you're so happy, but I thought you understood that when I told you of their offer last fall."

Happy? The teacher had no idea. It was the sign, the sign from the Lord. How could Mom not see it as the Lord's will now? Annie had tears start in her eyes. "I thought you'd forgotten. I thought I'd never get to go, not after Ben . . ." Annie broke off.

The teacher shifted in her seat, and her face reddened. "Well, there hasn't been any problem since," she said and coughed slightly. "Do you think you could press your mother for an answer? I know you've talked to her several times, but I think it's important that a decision be made soon."

Annie was ashamed to tell Miss Osborne how Mom was seeking a sign from the Lord. The teacher would think them a bit queer. "Mom's been thinking on it. She's noticed how hard I've worked."

Miss Osborne reached over and squeezed her hand. "It's all going to work out for you, Annie. When you did so well on the preexam, I knew my parents would be very impressed. Many pupils from the rural schools never get a passing grade on the entrance exams, but now and then there's someone like you, Annie—someone who excels without opportunities or exposure to cultural things."

They came in view of the house, and Miss Osborne turned her head slightly to look at Annie. "I'm proud of your commitment to learning, Annie," she said.

"Thank you. It was thoughtful of you to help me," Annie said, her voice thick with feeling.

Annie looked up toward the house as Miss Osborne turned into the driveway. Reverend Owens's auto was parked next to the house, and there was the strange quietness of no boys hanging on the porch posts or yelling and running out to meet them.

"Looks as if you have a caller," Miss Osborne said.

"Looks that way," Annie said, climbing from the Ford.

The teacher waved cheerily and drove off. Annie waved and started slowly toward the house.

SEVENTEEN

Annie stepped inside the kitchen. She set her dinner pail down and hung her sweater on the peg inside the door. She could just catch the murmur of voices coming from the parlor. Reverend Owens's voice boomed out suddenly, and there were peals of laughter. Annie smoothed her dress and stepped toward the parlor.

It wasn't that she disliked the preacher exactly, but he smiled too much; even when he preached a hellfire sermon he smiled, and he did have that certain way toward women . . . the weaker sex, he called them, grasping the sides of his pulpit and leaning forward with a wide smile that seemed directed only at the women of his congregation. "The downfall of man," he would say. Annie figured he might just as well say women were evil. It was clear enough to her that was what he meant.

The afternoon sun was slanting through the west windows, making the parlor pleasant and cheerful. Mom and the children were sitting on the davenport; the preacher seemed quite at home in the old rocker that had come down through Dad's family.

"Why, Annie, I didn't hear you come in," Reverend Owens said, leaning forward slightly, the rocker creaking on the bare wood floor. "I've been meaning to call on your mom, so I gave Ben and Leo a ride home from school today. We've missed you and your mother in church the last few Sundays. She tells me what a blessing you are." His smile was broad and as welcoming as at the opening of worship service. "How was the exam?"

Annie stayed in the doorway of the parlor. "It was fine, thank you," she said.

"Your good mother has been telling me that you've been studying to go to high school. It's important for young folk to have a vision. You know the Good Book says that without a vision the people will perish."

"Yes, Reverend. That'd be found in Isaiah," Annie said, pleased that he approved of her goals. His approval might make the Lord's sign even more evident to Mom. Annie looked her way, but Mom's eyes were fluttering with sleep.

"Goodness," Mom said with an embarrassed laugh. "I've about dropped off to sleep on you, Reverend." She eased herself from the davenport and struggled to her feet. "If you'll excuse me, Reverend, I really must be seeing to supper. The men always come in from chores half-starved."

"Yes, of course," Reverend Owens said. "You mustn't let them wait for their evening meal."

Annie turned to follow Mom and Grace into the kitchen.

"One moment, Annie. I would like a word with you about school," Reverend Owens said.

Annie turned back. She really shouldn't have thought such unkind things about him. He seemed to be truly interested in her schooling. Perhaps she would tell him about the Osbornes' offer. Annie quickly took Mom's place on the davenport.

"Will you tell us another fishing story when you're through talking with Annie?" Ben asked, hitching forward on the cushion.

"If there's time . . . but the school matter first," the preacher said, lacing his fingers together. He leaned forward and cleared his throat. "It has to do with your teacher."

"Miss Osborne," Annie said.

"Uh, yes, Miss Osborne," he said. "Recently I have learned of some unchristian practices she allows, perhaps even encourages, in the schoolroom."

"Miss Osborne unchristian? NO!" Annie shook her head. "Who . . . who would ever say such a thing?"

Reverend Owens flushed slightly and made large gestures with his hands and smiled. "Now, Annie, it is my duty as president of the school board and shepherd of my flock to listen to problems. Surely you understand that I cannot give out names?" he said, looking amused.

"But, but she has never done one thing . . ."

126

Reverend Owens rested his elbows on the arms of the rocker. "Perhaps not . . . perhaps it's been more than one thing," he said with a grave smile. "It's this, plain and simple, Annie and Ben. I've been given reason to believe that Miss Osborne isn't, well, upholding moral discipline. Do you get my meaning?"

No, she didn't get his meaning. Annie shifted her eyes to Ben. He seemed just as puzzled. Was he talking about the time Miss Osborne had given Ben a licking? Annie shook her head. "Why, Reverend, I've known Miss Osborne to thrash a boy when he needed it. I've not known her to have a problem more than once. The whole school is fond of the teacher," Annie said.

Ben and Leo nodded their heads in agreement.

"I see," Reverend Owens said, tapping his cheek. "Perhaps they are, but I'm concerned about her allowing such books as this in the schoolhouse." He pulled *Treasure Island* out from beneath his Bible. "I've been given to understand Miss Osborne lends out such books."

"Reverend Owens, *Treasure Island* has been on the bookshelf since I was in fourth grade. Mr. Adams brought it," Annie added swiftly, knowing that Reverend Owens had been a close friend of her old teacher.

The preacher wrinkled his forehead. "Oh? Well, I am more particularly interested in a certain poem in this book, the singing of which has been tolerated by the teacher for months. You are familiar with the poem?"

Annie looked at Ben. His face had gone white. She searched her mind for something to say. To just say yes seemed too obvious an admission of guilt.

"'Fifteen men on a dead man's chest,'" Reverend Owens said, drawing out the words. "'Yo-ho-ho, and a bottle of . . .' I don't think it necessary to repeat the whole poem to remind you what stand the church and the government of the United States have taken on the evils of drink. I would not want it to ever be said that our dear community was promoting such evil in its school-teaching, indeed, encouraging our children to go astray. Would you, Annie? Ben?"

"Please, Reverend. It's only a story . . . about pirates. The way they acted wasn't meant to be an example. Church folk know better about such things," she pleaded, aware that her fear and worry were showing through. She prayed that Mom would not overhear what was being said. But suppose the preacher had already told her?

Reverend Owens stood. "Don't fret, child," he said. "I would not hold you or your brother to blame for this. Clearly, the sin rests upon the person in authority. Truly, you know me to be a man of conscience, Annie." He reached down and patted her shoulder. "I'm deeply sorry if I've upset you, but the matter is settled in my mind." He swept his Bible and the book from the rocking chair. "I'll take my leave so you can assist your mother. Do care for your mother, Annie," he said, tucking the books under his arm.

"Yes, Reverend Owens," she said, seeing him to the door. He couldn't take his leave fast enough for her, but still she hurried to the window to watch as he drove from sight.

"I'll bet Justine Pruett is back of this, trying to get you . . . us in trouble—all on account of you going and calling her that name," Annie told Ben. "Well, she's done a fine job of things, more than she intended, I'd guess," Annie said, turning away from the window. She was chilled through with worry. What if the school board dismissed Miss Osborne? From the way the preacher talked, things did not appear too favorable.

"Annie?" Ben said, touching her sleeve as she started out to the kitchen. "What're we going to do?"

"Do? I don't know, Ben," Annie said. Oh, Lord, what would happen to her chances of going to high school if there were trouble now?

Eighteen

After supper that night, the younger children ran outdoors to play, and Dad and Russell carried chairs onto the porch. Pipe smoke and talk soon were drifting in through the screen. The sun had set, but still a lazy warmth lingered in the air.

Annie was scrubbing the pots when Mom came in and picked up a drying towel and started wiping the plates. Mom's color looked better this evening; she seemed to have a glow about her.

"What a pleasant surprise to have the preacher come calling. He truly is a fine man," Mom said, stacking the plates in the cupboard. "What was it he wanted to talk to you about, Annie? We were so busy with supper and then the men came in. . . . It was about school, wasn't it?"

"Mmmm . . . uh, yes," Annie said, banging the pot she was scouring against the metal dishpan. It appeared the preacher hadn't said one word to Mom about Miss Osborne. Annie was thankful to him for that much at least, but the thought of what could happen made her dizzy with fear. Reverend Owens might this very minute be proclaiming Miss Osborne unchristian and seeking her dismissal by the school board. "Uh . . . Mom, Mrs. Pruett will be stopping by this week. She's bringing a box of clothes and a sunshine basket. Justine said to tell you. I just this moment remembered."

"I was wondering, and it's none too soon. That Ben has sprouted up so, just the same as Russell did. Besides, I'll be needing the baby things." Mom pressed her hands over her stomach. "It's going to be this week. I'm sure of it."

"This week? Before Easter?" Annie said, hoping the baby wouldn't happen along before the Osbornes were to come.

Mom laughed. "After six babies, I guess I'd be knowing about such things. And to think Mae's starting in on a family already. There's things I'll be needing to tell her soon," she said, growing quiet. She stared out the window and wiped a plate over and over.

"Mom?" Annie drew a deep breath. "Mom, the Lord has answered our prayer," she began slowly. "Like Gideon's fleece, remember?" Annie set the last pot on the drainboard and faced her mother. "The Lord has sent his sign," Annie said forcefully, hoping she sounded like Elisha or one of the other Old Testament prophets.

"The Lord sent his sign?" Mom echoed, blinking. "Now why would you go saying that? The Lord has sent me no sign yet, Annie."

"This time the Lord sent his sign to me . . . this very day, through Miss Osborne. She told me on the drive home," Annie said, taking up a pot and drying it. "My teacher's folks are coming to see you the end of this week. They want me to stay with them so I can go to high school."

"Here, you say? They're coming here?"

"Yes, Mom, on Good Friday."

Mom seemed to lose her strength and leaned weakly against the cupboards. "Annie, the house is filthy dirty. You know it's not been spring-cleaned yet. The curtains and windows are black with smoke, and the floors haven't had a scrubbing since before Christmas. Annie, the Osbornes are not just neighbors stopping by. Whatever would they think of us? You know how particular I am, and we've had to let things go. Now don't go thinking I'm faulting you any; you've carried a load, but the Osbornes coming here?"

"Yes, but . . . it still is the sign we are seeking. You do see that it's the sign, don't you, Mom?"

"Might be. Might be. We'll see," Mom said.

"I could give the floors a scrubbing after school tomorrow, and the parlor windows aren't bad," Annie said. "I could tell Miss Osborne to bring her folks to the front door."

"The front door? Well, of course, they must come to the front door. I suppose I could make some tea biscuits. I've raisins enough, and there's the jar of mint jelly I was saving for Easter. . . ." Mom broke off. "I haven't forgotten how to be a lady," she said, straightening her shoulders. "My dad's side were always genteel-enough folk."

"That'd be the Martins," Annie said.

"Yes, of course, the Martins," Mom said. "Now get the step stool and fetch my grandmother's china tea set off the top shelf and my great-aunt Jennie's cut glass vases, and be careful," she said. "I know Erma Haines will be glad to share her jonquils. Her bank is just full this spring. We'll set the vases on the lamp-stands . . . we won't be needing the lamps. What a pretty sight those flowers will make. And, oh, the Victrola. We'll have a nice waltz, 'The Blue Danube,' or some record Mae got, playing when they are coming up to the door." Mom sighed. "Won't the parlor be inviting though?"

"Yes, Mom," Annie said, wishing she could get excited about the visit, but so many things could go wrong. She was worried enough about just meeting the Osbornes, and what she would say . . . and now there was all this trouble with the preacher. Lord, would she ever get to high school?

With the Osbornes' visit planned out by bedtime, Annie spent the night worrying about the teacher. The next morning as she prepared for school, she was glad to have her thoughts broken up by Grace's chatter about the Easter Bunny.

"And Ben and Leo said the Easter Bunny is big as a bear—big enough to look into our windows upstairs,"

Grace said, her eyes wide.

"Oh, what have those two been filling you with now?" Annie said, pulling on her sweater. "Grace, you know very well the Easter Bunny is a rabbit. They aren't big as bears." Annie checked out the south window; Justine was coming across the bridge, but she was alone. Aletha must have stayed home again. Even Leo and Ben wouldn't be in school today. Dad had taken them to help with plowing the cornfield.

"Walk with me far as Haineses', won't you, Grace?" Annie said with a sigh. The last person she wanted to be alone with was Justine. Annie was sure that Justine was the one who had riled up the preacher against Miss Osborne.

Grace scurried off to get her jacket, and they walked out to the mailbox to meet Justine.

Justine was unusually quiet, and her eyes were red and puffy. It appeared she'd been crying. Annie hoped she was suffering something fierce.

They had walked a short ways when Justine broke into sobs. "Something awful has happened," she said.

Grace's eyes went wide. "Did you get a licking?"

"Go back now, Grace," Annie said, giving her sister a gentle push.

"Justine did get a licking, didn't she?" Grace whispered.

Annie sighed. Grace would blab to Mom whatever it was Justine had to say, and it could be about the teacher.

"Annie, what are we going to do?" Justine said.

"Grace, hurry back now," Annie said. "I'll make you an Easter basket in school today if you hurry back . . . right now."

Grace looked with longing at Justine's teary face, but she turned and started toward home.

"Something dreadful may happen to the teacher," Justine said, beginning to cry again.

Annie was frightened. Suppose Miss Osborne was already dismissed? Justine would know; her father was on the school board.

Annie stopped and jerked Justine around to face her. "Stop it. Stop that crying," she said, shaking Justine. "Crying is not going to help the teacher one bit. Now, you best tell me what's going on, and if there's any remedy, I'll help—for the teacher's sake," she spat out, wanting to slap Justine. "Now come on," she said, pulling Justine down over the bank to the creek.

Annie rinsed her hankie in the cold water and thrust it at Justine. "Hold this against your eyes. It'll help the puffiness," she said gently. Even though she was shaking with anger, she didn't want to scare Justine into silence. "And now I want to know what's ailing you, and you'd best tell me the whole truth."

Nineteen

ustine held the cold wrung-out hankie against her eyes. "Promise you won't be angry," she said, still sniffling.

Annie crossed her fingers behind her back. "I promise," she said. It was something she hadn't done since she was maybe seven, crossing her fingers that way, but if she didn't promise, Justine would never confess.

"It was Ben . . . smashing my Christmas ball that way and calling me that awful . . . horrid name in front of the whole school. That's what started it," Justine said.

"But Miss Osborne gave him a licking. Wasn't that good enough for you, Justine?"

"Good enough? The whole school was laughing, making fun of me. Oh, what would you know about that?" Justine snatched the hankie from her eyes and glared. "Everybody loves you. Can I sit with Annie? Can Annie help me? Annie, Annie, Annie!"

Annie shook her head and stared at the creek water rushing past. Justine was jealous—of her—Annie Lucas.

"Justine, I've wanted for ever so long to be like you. Going on trips to town and buying hats and shoes and dresses in the store. You'll be going off to high school. Your folks have it all planned out for you; I wish it were that way for me."

Justine wiped her eyes. "You mean that, Annie?"

Annie looked steadily at her. "Why, Justine, you have a finer life than anyone I know. Now, you'd best tell me all you know about the teacher."

"Yes . . . about the teacher," Justine said. "You did promise not to be angry," she said, her eyes sliding away from Annie's face.

"Yes, I did promise," Annie said glumly.

Justine was breathless as she began. "I told my mother and father about how Ben never stops singing that song about the dead men and drinking. Father was upset, but Mother said . . . well . . . she said I was being foolish and to forget it. But I couldn't forget it," Justine said, pulling herself up straight. "So I told the Reverend last Sunday after church. He told me he would handle the matter. . . ." Justine's voice trailed off, and she twisted the hankie in her hands. "And then last night he stopped by and talked to my father."

"But what about Miss Osborne, Justine? What's going to happen to her?" Annie said. "What did he say to your father?"

"I . . . I don't know. I mean . . . I only know that Reverend Owens is blaming Miss Osborne for letting Ben sing that—that song. He's called a special school board meeting for tonight, and it's to be at our house, and, and . . . he went to see the teacher after he left our house. Annie, what are we going to do? I don't want anything bad to happen to Miss Osborne."

"Tonight? The meeting is tonight at your house?" Annie asked. She stood and brushed off the back of her dress.

"Yes, at my house," Justine said, struggling to her feet. "You hate me, don't you, Annie?"

"No," Annie said. But inside she was sick with worry. What would happen to Miss Osborne? "Justine, do you think Reverend Owens is right about the book? I mean, do you think *Treasure Island* is sinful?" she asked as they climbed up the bank to the road.

"I-I'm not sure. I do think it's wicked to drink. What do you think, Annie?"

"I don't hold much with drinking either. You know the same as me how some men don't take care of their families, and they let their farms run down on account of drinking. But I know of more than one man in the congregation that is not opposed to letting a jug of cider go hard. But *Treasure Island* sinful? No!" Annie said. "I suppose there might be shameful books written, but I've read some Dickens and George Eliot and Mark Twain, and I've read the Old Testament plenty. Seems to me they're all about the same."

Justine giggled. "Annie, how could you say *Huckleberry Finn* or *Treasure Island* was the same as the Bible?"

"Because they are," Annie said. "The books Miss Osborne lent me are about people, some bad and some good, just like in the Bible. And when I read those books, I start thinking about life and real people and how we should all be more caring about others; and it's wrong for anybody to say Miss Osborne is lacking morally for allowing us to read any book such as *Treasure Island*. If the board says we can't read the classics, then we should refuse to read the Bible as well!"

"Annie, you're wonderful!"

"No, not wonderful. If I had any guts, I'd stand right up and tell the preacher. . . . I would . . . but I don't," Annie said as they got to the schoolyard.

"Annie?" Justine tugged on her sleeve. "May I sit with you? Miss Osborne might be angry at me."

"She won't know you said anything. Reverend Owens wouldn't tell her that." But what if the teacher thought Ben was the one who had tattled? The Osbornes would never want a Lucas to board with them.

Annie gave the door a gentle push. It creaked open, and everyone looked up and stared as she and Justine walked in.

Miss Osborne turned away from the recitation bench, where the fifth graders were reading. "Hello, girls, I guess you were needed at home this morning," she said, smiling.

"Yes, Miss Osborne," they said. Justine slipped into

139

the empty seat beside Annie.

"You'll find your history lesson written on the board," Miss Osborne said, turning back to the reading group.

Annie opened her history book then and began reading the lesson. She glanced cautiously at the teacher for any telling signs, but Miss Osborne seemed calm and in good spirits, the same as she was any other day.

By the time Annie finished reading her assignment, it was recess. Normally Annie lingered in the schoolroom at recess until everyone had gone out so she could talk to the teacher, but today she and Justine hurried to go out. The teacher called to them just as they reached the door. "Annie, Justine."

Justine squeezed Annie's arm so tightly that she about yelped. They turned slowly to face the teacher.

Miss Osborne was by her desk. "My parents are coming on Good Friday," she said. "I would like to make the schoolhouse festive . . . bright with spring flowers and pictures by the children and some paper Easter baskets. I'd like the two of you to help me assemble materials for artwork this afternoon. . . ."

Annie and Justine looked at each other in surprise.

"Miss Osborne, didn't the preacher call on you?" Justine blurted out.

Miss Osborne laughed a bit too brightly. "Why, I guess he's been to see just everyone," she said, and her lip trembled. "I suppose this could be my last day of teaching."

Annie and Justine burst into tears, and the teacher wept quietly. She went to them and placed an arm on each of their shoulders. "Shhh . . . ," she whispered, the way a mother might. "I know you girls think only well of me. Now, let's be cheerful, shall we? The school board hasn't made a decision yet."

TWENTY

hen Annie and Justine got to the Lucases'
driveway after school that day, they saw the
Pruetts' auto parked by the back porch.

"You might as well come up to the house with me,"
Annie said with a sinking heart. She didn't mind
Justine's seeing the house, even though there was
plenty of clutter these days, but she was worried
about what Mrs. Pruett might have said to her mom.
"Do you suppose your mother said anything to my
mom about Miss Osborne?" Annie asked as they
walked toward the house.

"Mother's not one to gossip," Justine said. "But she
might say something about it. . . . The whole community knows by now, and . . ." She broke off and
stared at Annie. "You mean your mother doesn't know?
I thought Reverend Owens was here talking about it."

"He talked to Ben and me about it. Mom was off
making supper, and Grace was with her the whole
time, thank goodness. It doesn't matter. Mom or Dad
will find out soon enough," Annie said, wanting to cry.

When they got as far as the woodshed, Annie

dropped down on the chopping block. "Justine, there's something I ought to tell you," she said, kicking at the wood chips scattered on the ground. "The Osbornes are coming here tomorrow to visit us. They're going to ask my folks if I can board with them and go to high school, but if Mom finds out what Reverend Owens is saying about the teacher, she'll never agree to let me go. I've got to make my mom believe the preacher is wrong. . . ."

"Oh, no," Justine said, plunking down on the edge of the chopping block next to her. "It's all my fault, isn't it?"

Annie didn't answer. She turned away and stood up. "I can't stop thinking about the board meeting tonight . . . but, come on," she said, pulling on Justine's arm. "We'd better find out if my mom has heard. If she hasn't, then maybe there's still a chance. . . ."

"What? What are you thinking?" Justine asked, hurrying onto the porch behind Annie.

The white parlor curtains were fluttering on the clothesline. Most likely Mom would be worn out and cranky from the extra work she'd done to get ready for the Osbornes' visit on Friday.

"Justine, whatever I say about the preacher, *don't* agree with me," Annie said in a low voice. She pulled open the screen and they stepped inside.

Mrs. Pruett looked over at them and began to laugh. "I declare," she said. "You two look like you've been up to some mischief."

Annie laughed shakily and glanced quickly at Mom. She had latched onto the sunshine basket and didn't even look in their direction; Grace was napping in the big chair by the stove. "It's nice to see you, Mrs. Pruett," Annie said, nudging Justine forward to the table. "Have you been here long?"

"Why, no, dear, I just now got here myself," she said, sitting down at the table next to Annie's mom.

"Just look at this sweater set. It's a fine piece of work," Mom said, holding up the yellow crocheted clothes. "I'll bet Hattie Lester made it." She laid it to one side and reached back into the basket.

Annie and Justine looked at each other and shrugged. It appeared Mom didn't know; she didn't seem the least bit troubled.

"How did school go today, girls?" Mrs. Pruett asked. "How was Miss Osborne holding up?"

"What about Miss Osborne?" Mom said. "Something the matter with the teacher? She's not taking ill after I went and spring-cleaned the parlor all nice for entertaining her and her folks?"

"No, Mom," Annie said. "Miss Osborne is feeling fine." She picked up the baby clothes that Mom had set on the table. "It's just the color of jonquils and so soft," she said, holding the sweater set against her cheek.

Mom nodded. "And look at all these night sacks. The ladies worked extra hard," she said, fingering the flannel gowns and looking pleased.

"The Osbornes are planning to visit you?" Mrs. Pruett asked.

"Why, yes," Annie's mom said. "They want to talk to me about Annie going to high school," she said, looking proud.

"How wonderful! You will let her go, I hope," Mrs. Pruett said. "Really, you wouldn't let her miss such an opportunity, would you?"

Mom fixed her gaze on the new baby clothes. "It would be nice if she could, but there are things to give thought to, such as what the Lord's will might be. I have been praying about this, Mabel."

"Yes, yes, of course, Esther," Mrs. Pruett said, looking down.

"Umm . . . Justine . . ." Annie cast her friend a long look. "Ummm . . . did you happen to notice that *Treasure Island* was missing from the bookshelf in the school?"

Justine's eyes grew wide, and she shook her head as if Annie had taken leave of her senses.

"You remember when I brought *Treasure Island* home and read it to the boys, don't you, Mom?" Annie asked, leaning over her mother's shoulder.

Mom chuckled. "I should say so," she said, smoothing her hands over the stack of baby garments in front of her. "What a good time we all had with that. It kept the boys out of mischief for a good while, too."

"Well, Reverend Owens took it for himself that day he was substituting for Miss Osborne—you know, the day of the entrance exams?" Annie said, moving so she could watch Mom's face. "Mrs. Pruett, can you imagine that—the preacher reading about pirates?"

Mrs. Pruett shook her head. "These things happen," she said quietly, her eyes shifting from Annie to Mrs. Lucas.

Mom gave Annie a puzzled look. "I can't see why the preacher taking *Treasure Island* should bother you, Annie. There is no God-given reason saying he can't read something other than the Bible."

"That's right, Mrs. Lucas," Justine said. "I'm surprised that you would think such a thing, Annie."

"But . . . but, Justine, you know the same as me what drinking, thieving, evil men those pirates were . . . why . . . I think . . ." Annie broke off.

"You think that perhaps the classics wouldn't be fit for a preacher to read?" Mrs. Pruett raised her eyebrows. "I'm surprised you would have such closed-minded views, Annie. Clearly, the Bible gives us a realistic accounting of life . . . um, at times it's, well, rather vivid."

"I think you're being silly, Annie," Justine said.

Mom sighed. "I don't know what's ailing her today. Next she'll be saying that the *Christmas Carol* story isn't fit for reading either," she said and laughed.

"Then you think those books aren't a bad influence? They do speak of drinking. You know what the government and the church think of that," Annie said.

A shadow of doubt crept over her mom's face, and

Annie feared she had pushed her point too far. But she blurted out, "And . . . and just remember how Tiny Tim's family passed the jug around at Christmas and the Fezziwigs' party."

Mom slapped her palm down on the table. "Quiet yourself, Annie. I'll hear no more of your foolish talk," she said, her eyes watering. "You know full well my dear father loved that book and read it to me."

"Yes, Mom," Annie said, turning away. "I'm sorry if I upset you."

"Well, Esther, I'm pleased to see you are open-minded about the classics," Mrs. Pruett said, standing up. She looked over Mrs. Lucas's head and winked at Annie. "I guess we'd better be going now."

"I'll walk out with you," Annie said. It sickened her to think how she had tricked her mother, but still, she didn't want Mom to treat the Osbornes as if they were heathen and refuse their offer.

Justine latched onto Annie's arm and they walked out together as their mothers were saying good-bye. "Annie, you were wonderful," Justine said when they were on the porch.

"You and your mother were both a great help," Annie said. "But we have to think about the teacher now. Could you talk to your father before the meeting? Tell him how much you like Miss Osborne, tell him what a good teacher she is, ask him to vote in her favor, please?"

Justine nodded, but her face was sad. "Father

doesn't think the same way as Mother," she said as Annie walked with her to the auto. "But I will try. I promise you, I will try."

Annie waved to the Pruetts as they backed down the driveway, and then she hurried to the house. There was nothing to do now but wait for tomorrow. Even if Justine's father did vote for Miss Osborne, most likely the other board members wouldn't vote against the preacher.

TWENTY-ONE

W hen Annie stepped back inside, Mom was talking on the telephone. Quietly Annie edged toward the stove, her eyes flickering to the phone. She took up the galvanized pail from the floor beside the woodbox and dunked it into the hot-water reservoir.

Annie moved about the kitchen as soundlessly as she could. She hoped to learn what was being said, but Mom didn't seem to be talking, other than an occasional "That so?" Most likely it was Dad's cousin Madge, Aletha's mother, she was listening to. Annie could just imagine what Madge would be saying, going on and on in her sad, dull voice that always brought bad news. Was Madge telling Mom about the teacher? Had she kept Aletha out of school because of what the preacher was saying? Annie was sick with worry just thinking how cousin Madge might rile Mom up against the teacher.

Annie grabbed up the scrub brush and the soap and an old linen cloth and moved past Mom into the parlor.

"Yes, of course I'm still here, Madge, but I'll have to

get off soon," Mom said, her voice laced with a crossness perhaps only Annie knew well enough to catch.

There was no doubt that Mom was, this very minute, learning of the preacher's real intent for confiscating *Treasure Island* from the shelves at school. Annie could only throw herself into the work at hand and tremble.

She dropped to her knees in the corner by the front door and set about scrubbing the rough wood boards. It was a puzzle how so much dirt could settle in the cracks when the parlor was shut off for the greater part of the winter. Dad was always promising to finish off the floor, but Annie had never cared until now— now when the Osbornes would be walking through the front door.

Annie glanced back over her shoulder. When would Mom get off the telephone? What would she say about the teacher? Would Mom refuse to let her and Leo and Ben go to school, and would she call off the Osbornes' visit? Annie groaned and scrubbed harder on the floor.

Grace stood in the doorway, her cheeks flushed and hair rumpled from sleep. "Where's the Easter basket you promised to bring me?"

Annie sat back on her heels and pushed her hair away from her face with the back of her arm. "I forgot and left it at school. How'd you like to go with me tomorrow, hmmm?"

"All the way to school? Not just far as the Haineses'?"

Grace asked, coming closer.

"Miss Osborne said we could bring our younger brothers and sisters if they were school age come fall." Annie stood and tugged the davenport away from the wall and fell to scrubbing the floor behind it.

Grace's head appeared over the top. "Do I have to sit with you?"

"Annie?" Mom called from the doorway.

Annie stopped and raised up slowly. Already her back pained and her arm and shoulder ached. She peered over the top of the davenport. "Yes, Mom?"

"How much longer are you going to be?"

Annie studied her mom's face from across the room. Cold as creek water in spring, Mom could be, when she was irked. "I'll be done in no time at all, Mom."

"You'll have to get them curtains up by yourself, soon as the floor dries," Mom said. "Guess I'll be starting supper now. Grace, you come along and set the table and stop pestering Annie," she said, turning and leaving the room.

"Annie," Grace said, her voice low. "Can I sit with Mary Hathaway from church?"

Annie nodded. "If you promise to keep still during lessons."

"Grace, I thought I told you . . . ," Mom hollered.

"I promise," Grace said, sliding down off the davenport and skipping off toward the kitchen.

By the time Annie had scrubbed the blackened floor around the potbelly stove and moved the

Victrola away from the corner by the stairs, she was worn out. Finally Annie finished wiping the floor with the linen cloth and went out through the kitchen and tossed the water out the back pantry door.

"Go around to the porch and bring the curtains in off the line," Mom said, looking up from the cookstove, when Annie set the pail down. "Just one pair at a time, Annie, and be careful not to let them drag on the ground or get creased. There is no time to be wasted pressing out wrinkles. The Osbornes will be here tomorrow; there's plenty else for us to do."

"Yes, Mom," Annie said, hurrying out to get the clean curtains. It was a blessing that Mom still planned to entertain the teacher's parents.

Annie hung the sheer white curtains and straightened the furniture. Mom came in and cast an eye about the parlor. "It'll be passable enough after everything's been polished and the rugs beat and put down and the vases filled with jonquils." Mom shook her head. "It's a shame we can't depend on having a nice day. Good Friday, it always gets dark soon after lunch. That's when our Lord . . ." Mom broke off. "There'll be a thunderstorm. I can feel it coming. My joints don't lie."

"Mom, what did Cousin Madge want?" Annie asked as she followed her mother out to the kitchen.

"Why'd you want to know?"

Annie faltered. "Before . . . when you were on the phone, I thought . . . well, that something was wrong."

"Never mind that now. Maybe there was. Maybe you shouldn't be so nosy."

The kitchen door banged open, and Dad and the boys came in; their voices and thumping filled up the house with sudden warm cheerfulness. Annie hurried to help Mom take up supper while the boys washed in the pantry.

When they were at the table and the food was being passed, Mom sat still, her hands resting on her stomach, and gazed at the wall, her plate empty in front of her.

Annie could tell Mom was fasting and praying. They all watched her in uneasy silence as they ate, wondering what the cause might be.

Dad spoke finally, when he was cleaning the last of the gravy from his plate with a hunk of brown bread. "Thought I'd go to the coal flats tomorrow morning after barn chores are done and fetch up your ma," he said, shoving the gravy sop into his mouth.

Mom's face thawed. "That'd be right thoughtful of you, Warner. I didn't know how early you figured on going, but that does put my mind at ease," Mom said, touching Dad's arm.

"Will Grammie bring us peppermints?" Grace asked.

"She'll have too much else on her mind to be worrying about peppermints," Russell said.

"Soon as Mrs. Pruett left today, after bringing by the sunshine basket, your cousin Madge called." Mom paused and looked about the table, making sure she had the full attention of them all. "I have been pierced to my heart this day. . . . Cousin Madge told me how the preacher is fixing to get Miss Osborne dismissed at the school board meeting tonight. It is clear to me that he might just as well be fixing to rob me of my place as mother of this family, with the things he's been saying."

Annie's fork clattered to her plate as she stared across the table at Mom.

"What's this about Reverend Owens?" Dad asked.

Mom pulled herself up straight and looked from Annie to Ben. "He's been saying that Miss Osborne is an evil influence on our children by allowing them to read *Treasure Island*. I don't need to say who those children might be. He might just as well say the Lucases are evil. No telling what he'll get into his mind to say next. Most likely he'll be saying my dear *Christmas Carol* story is sinful. The very idea of it, Warner!" Mom gripped the edge of the table; her voice trembled.

"Now, Esther, don't get yourself all wrought up," Dad said. "You mustn't forget your condition."

"I'm not likely to do that," she said. "And I'm not likely to set foot in the church again until the preacher repents of the evil lies he's spreading about my children and the teacher."

Annie wanted to run around the table and give her mother a hug. If Mom took the teacher's part so strongly, surely she would see the Osbornes' coming and their offer as the sign from the Lord.

154

TWENTY-TWO

"Hold still, Grace," Annie said, her fingers shaking as she pulled the comb carefully through Grace's curls. She'd lain awake most of the night worrying about what was to become of Miss Osborne; this morning her stomach felt like one big canker sore. "Hold still," she said again. "I'll never get you presentable for school."

Grace stood in a kitchen chair and rocked against its back. "Will Miss Osborne let me read with Mary Hathaway, Annie? Can I take my primer? Mary told me in Sunday School that she takes her doll to play with at recess. Can I take mine, Annie?"

Annie sighed. "I'll see, Grace, but please stop rocking the chair," she said, glancing out the south window. Please be early, Justine. Oh, Lord, please let the school board vote in favor of Miss Osborne. She'd never get to high school if they made the teacher leave. It wasn't selfish or sinful to want something for herself so much, was it?

"Annie?" Mom stood in the doorway of the pantry. "Now don't forget to stop at the Haineses' on your

155

way home and get the jonquils. Let's see . . . Leo!"
Mom grabbed him by the collar as he was darting past
her in the doorway. "I thought I told you to take yourself down to the cellar and fetch me up the jar of mint
jelly. It says Mint Jelly right on it. It's on the window
ledge," she said, walking to the stove and setting two
irons down from the warming shelf onto the stove to
heat. "I'll get these doilies ironed and then mix up the
biscuits."

"Mom?" Annie pulled a violet ribbon from the
pocket of her pinafore to tie in Grace's hair. "Mom, do
you think the school board voted in favor of Miss
Osborne last night?"

Mom sniffed. "I couldn't say, Annie, but I prayed
about the matter, and we have to trust in the Lord. It is
written, 'All things work together for good to them that
love the Lord.' We'll just have to accept whatever
comes to pass."

Annie took a lock of Grace's hair and tied the ribbon into a bow. Why couldn't she accept things on
faith the way Mom did? But what possible good could
come of Miss Osborne's being dismissed? Miss Osborne
was the best teacher they'd ever had. Annie patted
Grace's head. "Run and get your primer now," she
said. "But you have to leave your doll home."

Grace stepped carefully from the chair. "Does my
hair look beautiful?" she whispered to Annie. Mom did
not take kindly to shows of vanity.

"Beautiful, Grace," Annie whispered back. "Hurry

up now or we'll be late," she said, taking off her pinafore. "Now don't get yourself all tuckered out this morning, Mom."

She wanted to ask her mother to change into Sunday clothes before the Osbornes came, but it wasn't the kind of thing Annie dared suggest. Most likely Mom would want to tidy herself, if she had time. "I'll hurry home from school to help. Miss Osborne said she'd dismiss us early, since it's Good Friday," she said, collecting her books from the sideboard.

Mom looked up from her ironing and smiled, tucking wisps of hair into her bun. "Don't fret now, Annie. I guess I can manage. You got most of the work done last night. There's just the biscuits to be mixed up. I'll rest for a spell after that."

Grace came downstairs with her primer and took Annie's hand. "Bye, Mom," she said. "I'm going to school now."

Annie tried to hurry Grace out to the mailbox, but Grace walked slowly, keeping her head stiff.

"Come on, Grace, stop worrying about your hair," Annie said, walking ahead. "Grace, would you please . . ." Annie broke off.

Justine was crossing the bridge. When she saw Annie, she waved her arms and broke into a run. "Annie! Annie!" Justine hollered.

Annie ran to meet her. She couldn't tell by Justine's voice if the news was good or bad. "Justine . . . ," Annie said. Unable to ask and fearful of the outcome, she grabbed her friend's arm.

Justine was out of breath. "Annie . . . Miss Osborne . . . they . . . they . . ."

"They what, Justine?" Annie burst out.

"Father says it's settled. The board voted for Miss Osborne to stay and to keep *Treasure Island*."

"Ohhh!" Annie whooped. "Ohhh! I can't believe it!" she said and burst into tears. It was the first right thing that had happened.

"Oh, Annie," Justine said, crying with her. "I'm so happy."

They laughed then, and Annie linked arms with Justine and they started back toward Grace. "So tell me, why . . . how?" Annie shook her head in wonder. How could the board vote against the preacher?

"After Mother and I left your house yesterday, I started thinking about how you said there were some men in the church that let jugs of cider go hard, and I recalled how my father had bought some whiskey cider over at Long Branch. He said it tasted real sweet, not like the hard kind. So mother and I came up with a plan." Justine started to laugh. "Oh, Annie, if only you could have been there. It would have been a true pleasure."

Annie smiled. Everything was turning out just right. "So tell me," she said, feeling the day to be truly glorious.

"Well, just when things were getting heated up real good against Miss Osborne, my mother steps into the parlor. 'Would you men care for some refreshment?' she says. And Father says, 'How about pouring us up some cider, Mabel.' And Mother says, 'Would that be the whiskey cider you wanted me to serve?' Father's face turned deep red, and the rest of the men, except for the Reverend, looked pretty shamefaced, too. And Mother says, 'Now, I want to know who's going to bad-mouth Miss Osborne and *Treasure Island?* It appears to me the pirates are sitting right here in my parlor.'"

"Your mother was so brave to call the preacher and all the board members pirates," Annie said. "I wish I could have been there."

"Annie!" Grace hollered out. She was walking toward them. "Hurry up; I've been waiting and waiting," she said crossly.

"What do you suppose the Osbornes will be like?" Justine asked as they continued on up the road.

"Oh . . ." Annie touched her hair. She'd had so many chores, and the worry over Miss Osborne on top of them, that she hadn't had time to fuss with herself. Her hair was flying every which way. She didn't know why she couldn't have hair like Grace. What would the Osbornes think of her? "I suppose they will be very nice," Annie said.

"Annie! Justine!" Miss Osborne called as soon as the girls came into view. She was waving and laughing. She must have heard the good news already. It was a pleasure to see her in such high spirits.

"You must be Annie," Miss Osborne's mother said, taking Justine by the hand when they got to the steps.

Annie winced and bent over to retie the ribbon in Grace's hair.

"Mother, this is Justine Pruett, and this is Annie Lucas," Miss Osborne said, laying a reassuring hand on Annie's shoulder.

"Oh, yes, yes." Mrs. Osborne nodded and fingered the lace on the bodice of her dress.

"And this is Annie's little sister, Grace. She's a visitor today just like you and Daddy."

Mrs. Osborne tilted Grace's chin. "Why, she looks just like a china doll."

"Yes, a china doll," Annie said, swallowing.

Mr. Osborne clasped Annie's hand firmly. "It is our pleasure to meet you, Annie Lucas," he said.

"Thank you . . . sir," Annie said, puckering the folds of her dress with her fingers. "It's a pleasure to meet you."

"Ben, why don't you ring the bell now? It's time for school to commence," Miss Osborne said, walking through the doorway.

Annie hung back. "Justine," she said, pulling her friend away from the group. "I don't think Mrs. Osborne likes me," she whispered as they went inside.

It was stuffy in the schoolhouse, and Miss Osborne had the boys prop open the windows to let in fresh air, but there was scarcely a breeze; flies and wasps buzzed on the sun-warmed sills.

160

"Boys and girls," Miss Osborne said, "we are in for a pleasant surprise today. It seems the school had a visit last night from the Easter Rabbit. Just look at what I found on my desk this morning." Miss Osborne held up an egg colored a lovely shade of rose. "He even wrote my name on it." She stopped and looked around. "Hmmm, I think we should forget about lessons this morning and see if the Easter Rabbit hid any eggs in the schoolyard."

There was a burst of happy shouts in the room, and the children ran out, laughing and calling to each other. Grace stayed in her seat. She stuck out her lower lip and glared at the desktop.

"Grace, what's wrong?" Annie asked, squatting down beside her sister. Couldn't Grace behave just for today? What would the Osbornes think? "Grace, the Easter Bunny came. Don't you want to hunt for eggs?" Annie said, wanting to yank her from the desk.

"You said I could read. You promised . . . ," Grace said.

"I'll stay in with her. I'll listen to her read," Mrs. Osborne said. "Would you like that, dear?" she asked.

Grace nodded slowly.

Mrs. Osborne clapped her hands. "Why, we can read and work on our letters and numbers. . . ." She looked at Annie and Justine and the teacher. "Shoo, the rest of you!" she said, motioning them away.

Miss Osborne and Justine and Annie walked toward the door. Annie glanced back at Grace. She was already sitting on the recitation bench with her primer open. "'The sky is falling . . . ,'" she was saying.

Annie sat down on the schoolhouse steps alongside Miss Osborne and watched as the kids raced around hollering and hunting for eggs. Maybe she shouldn't worry so much; Mrs. Osborne seemed taken with Grace . . . but Annie wasn't like Grace. She didn't look one bit like a china doll.

"My father hid the eggs early this morning," Miss Osborne said, shading her eyes and gazing at her father as he sported with the children. "He has this special way with children, you know. See how the kids have all taken to him?" Miss Osborne laughed. "Besides, he knows a few magic tricks."

Annie nodded. Ben and Leo and most of the other boys had gathered around him. He appeared to be putting a coin in his mouth and pulling it out of his ear.

"And my mother is—well, you probably noticed how nervous she is. It's just her way, and nothing for you to mind," the teacher said, reaching over and taking Annie's hand. "They're going to love having you stay with them. Don't worry, please?"

Annie nodded, a lump coming into her throat. She should have more faith. Hadn't everything worked out for the teacher? And weren't Miss Osborne's parents here to invite her to board with them? She really was a goose to worry so much.

"Oh, no," Justine said. She grabbed hold of Annie

and pointed down the road. A black Chevy had just driven into view.

"It's Reverend Owens," Justine said, her face turning red. "What shall we do?"

"We shall do nothing," Miss Osborne said. "We won't let him bully any of us, agreed?"

"Agreed," Annie said firmly, but Justine pressed closer to Annie and kept still.

Reverend Owens drove across the schoolyard and stopped his auto in front of the steps. "Warm for April, isn't it . . . ," he commented, wiping his face on a handkerchief before stepping from the auto. His manner was quiet, and his usual broad and welcoming smile was missing.

"Why, yes, Reverend Owens," Miss Osborne said cheerfully enough, raising her chin to meet his gaze. Annie could feel how tense she was.

Reverend Owens cleared his throat and coughed, raising a fist to cover his mouth. He appeared to be ill at ease, and Annie was surprised. She'd never known the preacher to be anything less than aggressive.

Miss Osborne kept her shoulders straight and stared at him. "Is there something I can do for you, Reverend Owens?" she asked in a pleasant, everyday voice.

"There is . . . yes . . . ," he said, inclining his head. "That is, there is one small matter I felt needed rectifying." He reached through the open window of the Chevy and brought out *Treasure Island*. "I believe this book belongs to the school. I'm returning it to you for the children," he said, holding the book out to her.

"Thank you, Reverend," Miss Osborne said, taking the book from his outstretched hands. "I'm pleased to accept this . . . for the children."

"Yes, well . . ." He cleared his throat. "A good day to you, ladies," he said, bowing slightly. He turned and climbed back into his auto and backed it out to the road. They watched as he drove from sight.

They were silent, staring after where he had been.

Finally Miss Osborne stood up and turned the book over in her hands, a look of wonder on her face. "Well . . . I guess I'd better call the children in. Daddy's going to be all worn out if I don't rescue him," she said.

Twenty-tHREE

T here were black clouds gathering in the sky
when Miss Osborne dismissed school at
noon.

"Tell your mother to expect us around one-thirty,"
the teacher said as Annie was leaving.

Annie pulled Grace away from Mary Hathaway.
Grace was acting all-important, tightly clasping the
schoolwork and drawings she had done. A body
would think no one but Grace had ever set foot inside a schoolhouse before.

"Grace, we have to hurry," Annie said. "We've got
to gather the jonquils for Mom, and it might rain."

Annie and Justine hurried Grace down the road. A
light wind was beginning to stir in the tops of the
trees and lift the red dust from the road into their
faces; already the air had gotten cool and damp.

"What do you think of Reverend Owens bringing
Treasure Island back to the teacher? I think he meant
it as an apology," Justine said.

"I was thinking the same," Annie said. "Still, I sus-
pect there's more to it than we know. I've never known

him to be meek to a woman before."

Justine nodded. "I'm glad this whole thing is over, and the teacher is staying, and you will be going to high school. . . . I'll miss you, Annie," Justine said. "It won't be much longer and we'll both be leaving South Branch, maybe forever."

Annie nodded. "We'll be home for holidays, and we can write to each other. Hmmm . . . I wonder what it will be like living with the Osbornes? I'll miss my family, I guess, but I won't miss scrubbing the outhouse or emptying slops," she said.

"I'd better head on home," Justine said when they got to the Haineses' yard. "It looks like it may pour. Good luck with the Osbornes and with your mom." She gave Annie's hand a quick squeeze before going off down the road.

"I wish Mrs. Osborne was my mom," Grace said, trudging beside Annie with her head down.

"Don't you ever say that, Grace Lucas," Annie said. She grabbed Grace by the shoulders and shook her. "Don't you ever go thinking you are better than your own kin. You hear me?"

"I don't care," Grace said. "Mom is fat . . . and dumb like Aletha."

"Don't you ever let me hear you say that again," Annie said. She was about to give another hard shake when Mrs. Haines called out and walked toward them.

"How's your mom feeling, Annie?" Mrs. Haines called as she walked across the yard to meet them. "I've been meaning to stop over. Tell her, if she needs help when it's her time, to have one of you run over and fetch me," she said. She began to help Annie gather the bright yellow flowers from the bank along the side of the house.

"Thank you, I will," Annie said. Grace sat on a rock with her back to them, her papers clutched in her hand. If Grace wasn't willing to pick flowers, most likely she would pout the whole day. Well, let her. As long as she didn't brag about Mrs. Osborne to Mom, Annie didn't care.

Mom was on the porch when Annie and Grace came up the driveway. "There's going to be a thunderstorm. What did I tell you, Annie?" Mom said, gesturing toward the eastern sky. "Good Friday it always darkens up this way."

Grace slipped right past Mom and into the house without saying a word. Mom didn't seem to notice Grace's strange behavior.

"Mrs. Haines said to fetch her if you needed help when your time came, Mom," Annie said.

Mom leaned against the porch post. She was breathing with her mouth open, and struggling to catch her breath. "That was real thoughtful of her, but I guess I won't be needing help now. Your dad took the team to fetch Grammie," Mom said. "And Russell loaded his stuff up in the Chevy this morning soon as chores were done. He set up the crib for me in his room before he left. He just can't wait to get started at that new job of his," she said.

"Mom, are you ailing?" Annie asked, fearful that Mom's time might be coming on now. Mom was still in her housedress and her hair wasn't combed. "Maybe, would you like me to do up your hair for you?"

"I am feeling poorly today," Mom said with a sigh. "It'd be a big help for me if you fixed my hair, Annie, but you go ahead and get them flowers in water while I change my dress. Then you can comb out my hair and tell me what those Osbornes are like. What are they like, Mr. and Mrs. Osborne?" Mom asked, following Annie into the house.

"They are real nice people, Mom." Annie stopped and looked at her mother's face, crinkled with worry. She dropped the jonquils on the table. "They're not one bit better than you," Annie burst out, wrapping her arms around her mother.

"There now, Annie. It never came into my mind that you might think the Osbornes were better than your own folks," she said, stroking Annie's hair. "Your dad and me are right proud of you, Annie. I want you to know that. You remind me so much of my own pa. You have that real caring for folk just the way he did."

Annie pulled back from her mother. "You . . . you think I'm caring?" she said, surprised that Mom saw her this way. She saw herself as being mean and selfish.

Mom chuckled. "Don't go getting a swelled head on you the way Grace has today. You know how I hate vanity."

"Yes, Mom," Annie said, grabbing up the jonquils and hurrying into the pantry with them.

Annie put the jonquils in the vases and set them on the lampstands in the parlor. Mom had put out the doilies and the crocheted chair sets; the red wood of the Victrola shone. The parlor had a pleasant homey look, and for once Annie was glad Mom was so fussy about the way things were cared for. After a quick glance around, Annie rushed up the stairs to her room.

She stripped to her waist and washed her underarms and sprinkled on some of the flower-scented talc the way Mae had shown her to do. She got up close to the mirror and tugged on her hair. Brushing it only made it stand out something awful. She wet her fingers and smoothed them down over her hair. She hoped Mom would see the Osbornes' offer as the sign from the Lord. What kind of sign would it take for Mom to know, if this wasn't it?

Annie shivered from the wind blowing in around the window frames. She reached into her bureau and got her sweater. Then she rushed downstairs to help Mom.

Mom had changed into the navy dress she kept for best. "I hope it doesn't start raining before they get here. Annie, where are the boys and Grace? I want them to stay on the porch and not go running off or in and out of the house, while the teacher and her folks are here. I'll be embarrassed to death if they start raring," Mom said, easing herself down into a kitchen chair. She handed Annie her hairbrush.

"I'll go out soon as I fix your hair and give them a talking-to," Annie said, brushing out her mother's hair and twisting it into a bun. "Mom, Reverend Owens came to school this morning. He brought *Treasure Island* back and told Miss Osborne it was for the children," she said, pushing the hairpins into Mom's bun.

Mom rested her arms on her stomach. "It all worked out for the good, just the way I prayed. Isn't that so, Annie?"

"Yes, 'all things work together for good to them that love the Lord,' just the way you said." Annie tucked a stray wisp of hair behind Mom's ear. Mom had prayed, and everything had worked out.

"I'll go out and talk to the boys now," Annie said, going to the screen door. The sky was completely overcast, but a strange orange light spread across the sky. Grace was sitting in an old chair on the porch. "Grace, have you seen Ben and Leo?" she said, going out onto the porch.

Grace didn't look up, and she didn't answer. Busily she kept coloring on the paper she'd brought from school.

"Just stay on the porch," Annie said. "Mom says she wants you to stay out here while the Osbornes are visiting. You hear me, Grace?"

Grace acted as if she didn't hear. She took a fat blue crayon and scribbled across the top of her drawing.

"Grace, if you disobey, I'll break every last one of your crayons."

Ben and Leo came tearing up the drive. "Hey, you boys come here," Annie called. "Mom wants you to stay on the porch and not go raring around when the Osbornes are here," she said when they got to the porch steps. "Besides . . . you can watch for Grammie Martin. I suppose she might be bringing you all something," Annie said loudly, sliding her eyes toward Grace.

"She will for sure," Leo said.

"Mom won't get mad if we play by the woodshed . . . Annie, please?" Ben asked. "There's nothing to do on the porch 'cept watch Grace act high and mighty."

"I guess," Annie said, looking at the black sky. Thunder rumbled close by. "You get yourselves up on the porch if it starts to pour." She went back inside and glanced at the mantel clock on the sideboard. It was one-twenty. The Osbornes might be here anytime and Mom was still sitting, almost asleep in the kitchen chair. "Mom?"

Mom's eyes fluttered and she sighed. "I guess I could use help getting out of this chair. Give me your hand, Annie," Mom said. "You'll have to serve the tea biscuits. I can't seem to catch my breath today." Mom bore down on Annie's arm and raised herself slowly from the chair.

Annie looked anxiously from her mother to the window. "I think I hear an auto. Maybe I'll just run and look," she said as soon as Mom was on her feet.

"Go ahead. I'll start on in. If it's the company, don't leave them standing outside. Have them come in, and don't forget your manners about it," Mom said.

Annie rushed into the parlor and pulled the curtain back to look. It was the Osbornes. They'd pulled up in front, the way Annie had said to.

"It's them, Mom," Annie called over her shoulder. A gust of wind blew Mrs. Osborne's dress up as she was stepping down from the running board. Annie saw the tops of her stockings; quickly she dropped the curtain. She hoped Mrs. Osborne hadn't seen her at the window. "Mom, you get the door, please?" Annie said, feeling afraid to face Mrs. Osborne. When Mom opened the door, Annie stood behind her.

"Please, come right in," Mom said. "It's brewing up some awful storm out there."

The Osbornes were no sooner settled in the parlor and properly introduced to Mom by the teacher when Dad pulled up with the team to the back door and the boys started hollering out to Grammie.

"This is very fine needlework," Mrs. Osborne said, fingering the doily on the arm of the davenport.

Mom was clearly pleased. "It's a design I worked out myself," she said, lowering herself carefully into the cushioned chair by the windows. "My, we'll be needing the lamps set out if it gets any darker."

Dad came into the parlor through the kitchen with Grammie and Grace right behind him. Grace marched over to Mrs. Osborne. "I've made you a drawing of Chicken Licken." She placed the paper on Mrs. Osborne's lap. "See, the sky is falling," Grace said, pointing.

Mrs. Osborne nodded and thanked Grace but didn't say one other word to her. Grace shifted her feet. She turned away, looking puzzled and about ready to cry; then she went over and crawled up on Grammie, who was now sitting in the old rocking chair.

Dad stood inside the doorway to the left of the stairway, his hat in his hand. "I hear you're offering to board our Annie so she can go to high school," he said.

"Why, yes, Mr. Lucas, that is the nature of our visit," Mr. Osborne said. "Our daughter has spoken so highly of Annie. We would be delighted to have her stay with us. We've been impressed by the schoolwork we've seen and by the maturity she's exhibited," he said.

Dad fingered the brim of his hat and looked thoughtful. "Annie, you want to go off to high school?" he asked.

"Yes, Dad, please?" she said.

"She's young to be going away from home, and she is sorely needed by her mother . . . but it seems like a real fine thing for her to do."

Annie wanted to leap from her place and hug him. Miss Osborne squeezed her hand.

"How do you figure it now, Esther?" Dad said.

"Seems to me the Osbornes' offer is a worthy one."

Mom pulled herself forward in her chair. "I've seen how Annie's studied and longed for more schooling, and it seems a right nice offer on these folks' part. . . ."

There was a sudden loud clap of thunder, and lightning split the darkened sky.

"I've been waiting on the Lord," Mom said. "And I figure you folks coming all this way is sign enough for me."

"Amen," Grammie said.

Annie sprang from her place and rushed over to her mother's side. "Mom, I, I . . ."

"Now, Annie, you know I can tell the Lord's own will, and, why not, it's clear as can be," Mom said.

"We're pleased you've accepted our offer," Mr. Osborne said. "We'll do our best to see that Annie's well cared for."

"I'd best get down to the barn and look after the livestock," Dad said, glancing out uneasily at the storm. He tugged on his hat and hurried out.

Mom struggled to pull herself out of the chair. "Annie, get those boys in here, and then you'd best trim the lamps," she said. "I'll get the tea things ready."

"Why don't you rest, Mrs. Lucas," the teacher said. "It's a real occasion for us to celebrate, and I would be delighted to give Annie a hand with her party."

Mom paused. It seemed she might allow it. "No, I wouldn't hear of guests waiting on themselves," she said, heading out of the parlor behind Annie.

Annie went through the kitchen to the back door. She gave a squeal of real pleasure and spun around. Lord, who would believe it? She was going to high school. She was going right out on the porch this very minute and shout it to the thunder and lightning.

"Annie." Mom called to her, but her voice was faint. "Annie!" Mom groaned.

Annie turned, her hand still on the doorknob.

"Annie . . . get . . . Grammie." Mom was panting, her face twisted with pain. She was clutching her stomach and leaning against the wall beside the window.

Annie stared, unable to move. Oh Lord, Mom was having the baby.

Twenty-four

om!" Annie was frightened by the pain on her mother's face. "Grammie, it's Mom! It's her time!" she cried as she rushed into the parlor.

Grammie pushed Grace off her lap and hurried toward the kitchen. "Annie, get the kids over to Mrs. Haines's," she said when she got to the doorway.

Annie stared after her. "Grammie knows what to do. Mom will be fine, won't she?" Annie asked her teacher. Her body felt heavy and unwilling to move.

The teacher touched her arm. "Annie, why don't you and the boys and Grace come on home with us?"

Annie longed to cry, to lean against the teacher for comfort, to run away with the Osbornes. Why did Mom have to have the baby now?

"I . . . I should ring up the doctor, I guess, and send Ben to fetch Dad," she said slowly, every word an effort. "Mom's in awful pain," she said, looking around at all their faces. "I guess I'll be needed here."

"There's always hard pain with birth, Annie," Mrs. Osborne said. "Don't upset yourself too much, dear.

176

I'm certain your grammie is very capable."

Annie nodded. Yes, Grammie knew about birthing.

"We'd best take the little one with us," Mrs. Osborne said, taking Grace's hand.

Mr. Osborne put on his hat and started for the door. "We'll round up the boys and send them to get your dad," he said.

"I'll stay with Annie," Miss Osborne said, seeing her folks to the door. The storm was beginning to pass over.

"Annie!" Grammie hollered out, just as the front door was shut. Her voice was filled with fear, and Annie rushed with the teacher into the kitchen.

Annie was chilled through when she saw Mom in the cushioned chair by the stove, her legs spread apart, her dress pulled up over her stomach. Mom screamed.

"Annie, hurry and ring up the doctor. We're going to need the doctor. It's coming feet first," Grammie said, kneeling down in front of Mom. "God, our Father in heaven . . ." Her voice cracked.

Annie rung up the operator. "Myrtle, it's Annie Lucas. We need the doctor real fast."

"Oh, hon, he's on his way to Clemos'. I put the call through not more than half an hour ago. I'll try to catch the doctor before he leaves there, hon. Hold on, now."

The Clemos lived just before the Perrys. The doctor could get here in just a few minutes.

Annie heard the Clemos' ring. "Avis, is the doctor still there?" Myrtle asked when the receiver was picked up.

The doctor took the phone. "Yes?"

Annie didn't wait for Myrtle but broke right in. "Dr. Atlee, it's Annie Lucas. It's my mom. My grammie says the baby's coming feet first. She's bleeding something fierce."

Mom screamed.

"You keep calm. I'll be right there," he said.

Annie hung up the phone. "He's on his way." Miss Osborne was wiping Mom's forehead.

"There's too much blood," Grammie said. "He'd best get here fast."

Dad came in. He looked over at Mom, his face going white. "Did somebody ring the doc?" he yelled. "Esther!" he cried out when she screamed.

"It's you that's to fault for this," Grammie said. "You men, always going at it . . . selfish, not caring one bit. Well, Warner, you might lose her this time." Grammie's voice was sharp. "I want you out of here. You've done damage enough."

Dad backed away. The doctor drove up then, and Dad hurried out to meet him. Dr. Atlee came rushing in alone and sent Annie and Miss Osborne into the parlor and closed the connecting door.

As Annie passed by the parlor window, she caught sight of Dad, his head bent, an arm around each of the boys, walking in the drizzle down the path toward the barn. Had the boys heard Mom screaming, heard Dad being tossed out that way by Grammie?

"Is Mom going to die?" Annie asked, turning away from the window and staring at the closed door to the kitchen.

Miss Osborne shook her head. "Annie, dear, the doctor knows about this kind of birth. Your mom should be fine," she said, taking Annie by the hand and leading her to the davenport.

Annie sat down on the edge of a cushion. She didn't know one thing about birthing matters; she'd always been sent away before. But it was going badly for Mom. She'd seen that in all their faces, the urgency, the fear—and what if Mom died? Annie shuddered. She could never leave home till Grace and the boys were near grown. Please don't let Mom die, she prayed. Forgive my selfish ways, oh Lord. But please don't let my mom die.

The afternoon wore on. Annie and Miss Osborne sat on the davenport not speaking, their eyes on the parlor door, listening for what was taking place. The rain let up finally, but the wind kept on with its constant whining. There had been no sounds from the kitchen—no moans or screams, no word from Grammie or the doctor to ease the fear.

Dad came up to the front door, his face scared and beaten. "How's your mom, Annie? Any word?" he asked. He came in and stood, awkward and solemn, just inside the door as if he were a stranger.

"No word, Dad," Annie said, longing to comfort him in some way, wanting some comfort for herself.

There were footsteps weary and slow in the hallway. The three of them turned toward the kitchen door. Annie held her breath. *Please, oh Lord, I'll do anything Mom wants, just don't let her be dying.* The teacher gripped her hand.

The knob turned slowly, the door opened, and the doctor came into the room and closed the door behind him. He removed his glasses and stood, his head resting against the door, his eyes closed. He let out a great sigh. "It's over. The baby, a girl, is fine. The mother is weak, very weak." He opened his eyes and looked at them. "Her condition is not stable. She lost a great deal of blood. Is there anywhere the younger children can stay for a few days?"

"Grace can stay with me," Miss Osborne said.

Dad blinked and stared at the floor. "The boys can go next door to the Haineses'."

"We'll have to move her into the bedroom. She mustn't have any callers, and she won't be able to nurse," he said, looking at Annie. "She's very weak. It will be a good long time before your mother gets back all her strength."

How long? Annie wanted to ask, but she was ashamed of her selfish thoughts. How long was a long time? A week, a month, a year? Too long for her to go to high school?

Twenty-five

nnie stood in the doorway of her mother's bedroom. It was a warm spring morning; Grammie had raised the window, and a soft breeze was parting the curtains. Clear light touched the room.

It had been a week now that Mom had lain ill and not in her right mind. Grammie had come from the room that morning weary but praising the Lord. "She's fought a good fight, and she's won. She's asking to see you. Go on in now. Take the baby with you."

"Mom, Grammie said you wanted to see me."

Mom's eyelids fluttered. "Annie?" Mom smiled and beckoned with her hand for Annie to come near. "Show me my baby," she said.

Annie stepped over to the bed and placed the baby in Mom's arms.

Mom brushed her fingers lightly over the soft down on the baby's head. "Katie, my little Katie, what a beauty you are, same as all my babies," she crooned, her voice sweet.

Annie wondered at the glow on Mom's face.

"Annie, has she got all her fingers and toes?"

"Yes, Mom."

Mom sighed. "Grammie says you're a good mother and a real blessing, Annie."

"It's not been a real chore caring for the baby. She's a good sleeper and quiet as can be, not like Grace was, all the time fussing and crying."

"Grace and the boys, Grammie says they're not here. When are they coming home? I want all my children here."

"Soon, Mom . . . soon as the doctor says."

"My arms are tired, Annie. Could you lay Katie on the bed beside me? Maybe you could bring the cradle in here, now that I'm on the mend."

"Yes, Mom," Annie said, moving the baby from Mom's arms onto the quilt. "Mom . . . I prayed real hard for you to get better." Annie leaned over and kissed her mother's cheek. "We couldn't get on without you." She felt guilty remembering how her first thought had been of herself—the fear that she wouldn't get to high school after all.

"There now, Annie," Mom said, looking pleased. "The one thing I always know is that my Annie loves me—more than the others do. I know that."

"Oh, Mom," Annie said, tears starting in her eyes. What would Mom think if she knew *all* that her Annie had prayed for? "You'd better rest now."

Mom nodded and closed her eyes.

Annie went back through the parlor. She noticed how the yellow jonquils had faded and gone brown. She picked the vases from the lampstands and carried them into the kitchen.

Grammie was standing with her back to the stove. She shook her head when Annie set the vases on the table. "My, how we've let the chores go. I noticed just this morning how the floor was gritty under my shoes. We'd best do some sweeping and clear up some of our clutter, now that your ma's gaining. She'd have our hides if she saw this kitchen."

Annie sat down in Dad's chair at the table. "Grammie, Mom is weak. . . ."

"That she is, girlie."

"I've been wondering . . . I mean, you know about women and birthing and all. I suppose Mom might not be getting around much for, oh, maybe a month."

"That'd be about right, I guess," Grammie said.

"Are you, can you stay that long, do you think?"

"I figure I can stay till school's out, but I can't stay away from my work longer than that. I have my own needs to take care of. It's only because I've worked for Woodmansee's so long that they were willing to spare me. Your ma's got you to see to meals and such."

"Yes, that's true," Annie said. "The doctor said it'd be a good long time before Mom had her strength back. How long might that be, Grammie?"

"She'll be frail for leastways a year, I'd figure. Oh, she may get to looking better, but don't go taking that as a sign she's able to do heavy work. It won't be so, and if she gets in the family way again it'll be the end of her for sure," Grammie said, trembling with anger.

Mom might be poorly for a year. She might never get better. It seemed there was no way of telling, and Annie wanted to cry. Mom had said she could go to high school, but how could she do that now? Annie stood and walked over to the cradle beside the stove. "I'm going to take this in by Mom. She's wanting the baby near her," Annie said, lifting the cradle and carrying it out.

Later on that afternoon, when Mom and the baby were sleeping and Grammie was napping on the davenport, Annie slipped outside and sat in the old rocker on the porch. In just a week's time, the red of budding trees had sprinkled the hillside with color. The pasture grass was green now, and Dad had turned the heifers out to graze.

Annie set the rocker in motion and stared up the valley past the Haineses' to where the road disappeared from view. If only she could get back to school soon. There were only a few more weeks before summer recess, but it wouldn't be right for her to leave Grammie with so many chores until Mom was able to take over caring for the baby. It seemed as though they were living in a quarantined house, with no one being allowed to call on them. Dad came in only for meals, and it tore at her something fierce to see him looking so sad.

The sun was warm, and Annie felt her body going limp with sleep. She was so weary from all the work and worry of the past week. She was startled from her near-doze by the sound of an auto turning into the drive.

It was the teacher with Grace. Annie sprang from the rocker to meet them. Grace broke from Miss Osborne's side and ran up to the house. "Annie!" Grace cried, throwing herself into Annie's arms. Annie pulled her close; Grace buried her face in Annie's neck. "I cried. I wanted you, Annie," Grace said.

"I saw you on the porch, and I had to stop. We've all been worried," Miss Osborne said, coming up the steps. "How is your mom?" she asked, studying Annie's face.

"Just this morning she's come around. She's weak, but she'll be gaining now."

"What's going on here?" Grammie asked, poking her head out. "Why, it's the teacher bringing Grace. Your ma's been begging to see you, little lady. Come in now and get a look at your new baby sister and see your ma."

Grace hurried into the house as soon as Annie put her down. "Can I hold the baby, Grammie, please, can I? I've been waiting and waiting," Grace said as she disappeared from sight.

"Have the boys been behaving in school?" Annie asked.

"They're fine, but homesick, I can tell. They've been

wearing the longest faces and hanging onto Grace—
I've been bringing her to school with me. . . . I guess
they'll be coming home now."

"I guess," Annie said. She longed to say what was
on her mind, but it was hard to begin.

"I've got your scores from the entrance exams. I was
so proud and thrilled when I saw them, Annie." Miss
Osborne took an envelope from her handbag. "They're
awarding you a diploma because of your outstanding
performance. This is truly an honor," she said, opening
the letter and handing it to Annie.

Annie stared at the row of A's. Her eyes blurred,
and suddenly she burst into tears and let the letter
drop from her hands. She walked to the end of the
porch, away from the open door.

"Annie, tell me, what is it? What's wrong?" Miss
Osborne asked, coming up behind her.

"I-I can't go to high school," she managed finally,
turning to face her teacher.

"Annie, whatever do you mean? It's all been decided. Your parents have agreed. Your mom even
gave it the Lord's blessing, and she's getting well.
Everything has worked out for you just as I knew it
would, hasn't it?" Miss Osborne said.

Annie shook her head. "Grammie says Mom won't
get her strength back for leastways a year. She says the
heavy work will be too much. How can I leave now? I
want to go. The Lord only knows how much."

"But the boys, surely they could help out."

"No, Dad needs them in the barn and to work in the woods with his logging in the winter, now that Russell's gone."

"There must be a way. We'll think of something," Miss Osborne said.

"I've seen how Mom's strength was sapped away even before the baby came, and now with her almost dying . . ."

Miss Osborne put a hand on her shoulder. "Annie, maybe you are right. But you mustn't give up your dream," she said, turning Annie around to face her. "Don't ever give up your dream."

Twenty-six

I t was the last day of school. They had a picnic outside under the trees and all sorts of games, but even with the festivities and high spirits, Annie couldn't forget that this might be her last day of school for a long time to come. She stayed after and helped the teacher clean up and pack her things.

"I will miss teaching here and the children, but, Annie, I will miss you most of all," Miss Osborne said. She looked up from sorting through her desk drawer and gazed about the schoolhouse.

"What do you mean? You'll only be away for the summer, won't you?" Annie asked. She was kneeling on the floor at the back of the school, clearing Miss Osborne's books from the shelves and putting them in a box.

"I'm afraid not. I've decided to continue my studies at the college," the teacher said.

"I see," Annie said, getting to her feet and carrying the box to the front. "I guess your folks are happy."

"Y-yes, it's what they wanted all along," Miss Osborne said. "I would've continued teaching here, but so much has happened, you know."

Annie set the box down on the desk. "But Reverend Owens has announced he's leaving, and the children like you so much, and Grace . . . I thought you would be her teacher, and I was hoping to see you sometimes myself."

Miss Osborne shook her head. "I can't stay, Annie. Sometimes . . ." She stopped talking and stared out the window. "Sometimes life is so unfair. Sometimes it seems as though others determine our destinies. Sometimes we seem to have little choice in what befalls us."

Annie ran her finger over the gold lettering of the Bible that was on the teacher's desk. "'Like a wave of the sea driven with the wind and tossed . . .'" she said softly, blinking back tears.

It was quiet a moment before the teacher spoke. "Please, let me give you something . . . something to remind you of our good times together." She pulled open the bottom drawer of her desk. "I've wanted to give you this for the longest time. Here, hold this to your ear, Annie," she said, thrusting the large conch shell into Annie's hands. "Remember that day in school? The poem you wrote. It went . . . um . . ."

"'Let's stroll along by the ocean,'" Annie said, holding the shell up against her ear, "'by the white and sandy beach. . . .'" She could hear the ocean now; the waves were roaring in her ears, filling up her head with wonder.

* * *

The summer passed slowly, and Mom didn't gain much. Annie was troubled to see her mother so weak. It seemed every few days she was down in bed with some ailment. Mom would fret that she was putting too much on Annie's young shoulders; Ben and Leo had taken over Russell's chores, and Annie had no one to help her with the heavy work. She struggled to keep the house the way Mom liked it, but she never could get caught up. There was the bread to be made fresh every day and the meals and the gardening and the wash. Grace helped her when she could, and baby Katie never fussed much.

Finally the biggest share of the canning was done and school had started again. It was hard for Annie to watch the boys and Grace going off mornings. How she longed to go with them, even if it wasn't high school. She looked forward to evenings when the supper dishes were done and she could sit at the kitchen table and help Leo with his reading and spelling and Ben with his arithmetic. It was almost the same as being a real teacher.

"Annie, would you walk far as Haineses' with me this morning?" Grace asked, watching as Annie packed the dinner pails. "Ben and Leo won't ever wait for me, and I don't have nobody to walk with. Please, Annie?"

"Anybody, Grace. You don't have anybody to walk with." Annie sighed. "I guess I can go," she said.

Already the September morning was growing hot

when she and Grace started up the road. As soon as she left Grace, she was going to go blackberrying up on the old Lester place.

She'd had such a longing to get off by herself ever since yesterday, when she had gotten a letter from Miss Osborne. Annie had read it over and over, until the words were inscribed on her heart.

> *My Dear Annie,*
>
> *How much my thoughts have been with you since school has commenced; how much I long to see you going on with your education. I visited my old high school a few days past and was able to procure a couple of textbooks for you. I'm afraid they are rather battered, but I know you will treasure them and that they will give you many hours of pleasure just the same. Remember that you have a home here with me and my parents whenever you feel free to leave your mother. I believe in you, Annie. You must never give up. . . .*

Aletha was already hanging out wash at the Haineses' when Annie and Grace came along. Aletha had taken up housekeeping at the Haineses' in July, and sometimes Annie walked over to visit with her in the afternoons when Mom and the baby were napping. She should probably ask Aletha to go berrying. Mrs. Haines wouldn't mind letting her off for the morning, but today Annie wanted to be alone. She waved to Aletha and started back to the house, not watching Grace go out of sight as she did some days.

Annie grabbed the berry pail off the porch and started off down the road. Today seemed much the same as the day she had gone off for the luncheon. She had been happy that day, having tea and Mom's elderberry jelly with Miss Osborne. "You have a great deal of potential," the teacher had said. "I think you should go to high school." Annie hadn't ever considered it. But now she thought about it every day. What new things would she be learning if she were in high school? It seemed the whole world was moving on without her.

Annie stopped before she got to Justine's and cut through the Hathaways' field and up over the hill. She didn't want to walk past the Pruetts', not because she was afraid Justine might see her old brown shoes, but because Justine wasn't there. Annie missed her more than she ever would've guessed. They'd become so close the past few months. But Justine had gone to board with her aunt in Poughkeepsie to start high school.

Annie crossed over the creek bed. It was nearly dry this year, and she stepped across it on the stones. She set about picking the berries on the Lester place; the blackberry briers had grown up along the old barn foundation and hidden the caved-in rotting boards and rusted scraps of old tools and broken machinery.

She was soothed by the sounds of late summer, the grasshoppers whirring in the tall dying grass of the forgotten field. Such peace. She picked around the back of the foundation and came out to the front, where she could see the road again. She shaded her eyes and gazed out past the tumbledown Lester house to the Perrys' across the road. She'd picked nearly all the ripe berries; her pail was plenty full enough. It wouldn't hurt to just go over there and think about the day she'd spent with the teacher. She'd go home by the road then instead of taking the shortcut. She wasn't in a hurry to get home; it wouldn't be noon for a good while yet.

She walked out across the field to the edge of the road. She wished it were last year again. How sweet and wonderful those days of dreaming seemed now. She had the notion that Miss Osborne might appear, that even as she turned away and walked the road down over the hill, the teacher would be watching her from the Perrys' porch. When she got to the top of the first rise, Annie turned slowly. Miss Osborne wasn't there, but Annie raised her hand in a wave just the same before starting down over the hill out of sight.

She was down the road almost to the Laytons' when a horse and wagon came up behind her. She stepped off the road and walked along, her skirt brushing against the dust-covered goldenrod. It was probably a farmer taking the morning's milking to the creamery. She wished they'd get on by her, but the horse was

193

reined to a stop. "Hey, there—Annie Lucas, isn't it?" a friendly voice hailed.

Annie looked up surprised and embarrassed. The farmer was Lee Mosher.

"I'm on my way to the creamery. You might as well climb up and ride with me," he said.

Annie hesitated, her face growing warm. What if he taunted her, asked why she wasn't in high school. Well . . . it would be rude not to accept a kindly offer.

He wrapped the reins in his hand and leaned over. "Just give me your pail," he said, holding out his hand. She did so and climbed up beside him on the wagon seat.

She sat with her back stiff, feeling uneasy with their closeness.

Lee set the berry pail down behind them in the wagon bed next to the cans of milk and urged the horse on. "My father says your folks have another baby. We were sorry to hear your mom had such a bad time of it."

"Thank you," Annie said meekly. She should have known he would understand why she wasn't in school.

They rode in silence for a time.

"How were your grades on the entrance exams?" Lee asked finally.

"Quite good," Annie said primly.

"I bet you got all A's—you got all A's, didn't you?" he said with a laugh.

Annie smiled. "Yes, I did," she said.

"So, you *were* the one! I was right." He laughed. "My teacher said some girl from your school got the highest grades. So I guess that makes you the top pupil in the district. I'm glad it was you and not that prissy one."

"Thank you," Annie said. She took a deep breath. "So, how did *you* do?"

"Well, I got A's, of course . . . and B's," he added.

They both laughed, but then Lee grew quiet. "I'm sorry things didn't work out for you to go to high school," he said. "But if you're ever looking for a housekeeping job, we'd be pleased to hire you come next haying season."

"It's kind of you to offer," Annie said. "But I'm still planning to go to high school if . . . when Mom gets back her strength. My teacher is sending me some high school books to study, and her parents are willing to board me when Mom is better." Annie stared down at her hands.

"Why, Annie, your mom is sure to get better, and a year is no time at all." He stopped the wagon along the edge of the road near the creamery. "Wait, Annie," he said as she started to climb down. He reached down and pulled something out of his pocket. "Remember the arrowhead I found the day of the exam?"

"Yes," Annie said. She remembered she hadn't gotten to look at it.

"I've carried it with me ever since, but I'd like you

to have it for good luck—if you'll take it." Lee held the arrowhead out to her.

"I've always wanted one. . . ." Annie hesitated. "If you really want me to have it . . ."

"Here, it's yours," he said, pressing the arrowhead into her hand.

"Thank you, Lee Mosher," she said, closing her fingers over the relic. "I'm sure it will bring me good luck." She climbed from the wagon, and Lee handed her down the berry pail.

"We'll meet again, Annie Lucas; wait and see if we don't," he said.

"I hope so," Annie said. Then she turned and started walking toward home, her face lifted to the sun.